LUELLA'S LONGING

ROMANCE ON THE OREGON TRAIL BOOK TWO

KATHLEEN BALL

This book is dedicated to all the Grandparents that are helping to raise their grandchildren. It can be exhausting but they add so much love and joy.

And as always I dedicate this nook to Bruce, Steven, Colt, Clara and Mavis because I love them.

CHAPTER ONE

*D*eclan Leary stretched his back as he held the lines. Driving oxen all day was boring and all the bumping and jostling was uncomfortable. He'd drawn the short straw that morning. Heath and Zander had laughed. They got to be drovers and make sure Mr. Walsh's cattle and horses made it to Oregon.

When they signed on they expected to work for almost nothing even though they had a contract. Declan and his brother Heath had been in America for a year and hadn't been treated honestly yet. Until now. Until Mr. Walsh had hired them.

He swore the bumps were getting bigger. He thought people were supposed to make sure there weren't too many rocks on the trail. Breaking a wheel or axel could set them back a good while. A loud scream erupted from somewhere up ahead, and the wagon train was slowing to a stop. He strained, trying to hear what was happening. It sounded like a woman wailing.

He set the brake and tied off the lines before he jumped

down. Three wagons in front of his passed in a blur as he ran. A crowd was forming at the side of the Barnes Wagon.

"See anything?" his boss Harrison Walsh asked.

"No, but I know I heard a female scream. I bet it's Luella. She's always getting into trouble."

Harrison's wife, Cora joined them. She was holding their baby, Essie. "Has Mrs. Chapman taken charge yet?"

"I done tol' her and tol' her not to jump off the wagon when it was movin'," Auggie Barnes roared at his wife Ebba. "Now she's worthless. It might be a blessing if the good Lord just took her."

Declan made his way to the front and spotted Luella on the ground, one of her legs red and raw like nothing he'd ever seen. Even as she howled and sniffled, she was tugging at her skirt, trying to cover her exposed leg. Declan shifted his gaze, since it wasn't considered proper for a lady to show her legs, and it seemed a lot worse for him to stare.

Mrs. Chapman, the only one on the train who knew about medicine and healing, was trying to get Luella to drink something. But Luella kept shaking her head and struggling with her skirts.

Declan went down on his knees. "What can I do to help?"

"Get her to drink this laudanum," instructed Mrs. Chapman in a brusque tone. "I will try to examine her leg and it's going to hurt something awful. The rest of you, I need splints and bandages."

"Hi Luella, I guess you took a fall." Declan smiled gently at her. He'd had a sister until she starved to death at a young age, and now he found himself with a soft spot in his heart for helping others. "I know a lot about pain, and the one thing I've learned is if there is a way to dull the pain, do it. Mrs. Chapman fixed up my friend Zander. You remember that, don't you? Drink this and we'll get your leg straight and then I'll lift you up into your wagon."

"Oh no, someone else will have to take her or we leave her," Auggie said. "She is disobedient and lazy. She'd be more trouble than she's worth."

"Auggie no," Ebba cried. "She's our daughter."

"Is she?"

Ebba gasped and stalked off without another word.

Cora handed Essie to Harrison and kneeled down next to Declan. "Take my hand, Luella. Your parents are just upset at the moment. Everything will work out, you'll see."

"Thank you," Luella managed to croak out. She glanced at Declan and nodded her head.

He held her shoulders up and helped her to drink the water laced with Laudanum. "It works fast." He lowered her back down and smiled at her. No one had even gotten a blanket to cover her. What was wrong with people?

"Mr. Barnes, will you get a blanket for her?"

The rage on Auggie Barnes' face surprised Declan. "She gets nothing from me. Her only worth was to make a good marriage to a man with money. Now look at her. She'll never walk again. She'll be a burden for the rest of her life."

Harrison joined them a few minutes later with two blankets. He handed one to Declan and rolled the other one up and put it under her head.

"Thank you, Harrison," Mrs. Chapman said. When people brought the necessary supplies, she glanced up at Declan. "Hold her still, you too Cora." She pulled until the leg looked straight again. With one heart-wrenching scream, Luella was out.

"We need to move her to her wagon," Mrs. Chapman said after she splinted the leg and wrapped the splints with bandages.

Auggie stood at the back of his wagon with his rifle cradled in his hands. "I said no."

Declan wanted to use his fists on him but settled for giving him a look of disgust instead.

Mrs. Chapman stood. "Surely one of you has room in your wagons. I'll tend to her." She looked at the crowd.

Every one of them avoided her gaze, some staring into the distance, others studying the ground as they kicked dirt and shuffled their feet. No one spoke up with an offer of help.

Mrs. Chapman shook her head. "I don't know what to do, Cora." Mrs. Chapman was usually so good in a crisis, but now she looked as though she wanted to cry.

The captain elbowed his way to them. Captain London stared at Auggie. "You sure about this? It's an awful thing to do to your daughter, and I don't want to hear your theory that she isn't yours. She's the spitting image of you. If you don't take her into your wagon now, you won't be able to take her back once she can do chores again."

"She'll never mount to anything now," Auggie sneered. He tightened his hold on his shot gun.

"Cora, take Essie. I'll make room in the extra wagon." Harrison handed the baby to Cora. "It'll take me a minute to get the wagon ready, and then I'll be back to help carry her."

Captain London nodded.

Declan suddenly became aware that he was smoothing back Luella's fair hair off her face. He stopped quickly and glanced around. No one seemed to think anything about it except for his brother Heath and their friend Zander. From the expressions on their faces he'd be in for some joshing later. He gave them his best glare and they both smiled at him.

"Declan, can you get her head and shoulders, Captain how about you take the middle and I'll hold her legs straight?" Harrison suggested.

"Fine, let's get her there before she wakes up," the captain said as he got in place.

Harrison counted to three and they all lifted at the same time, slowly and carefully carrying her to the wagon Declan had been driving.

"I'll ride in the back for a bit," Mrs. Chapman said.

Cora smiled. "Let me know when it's my turn."

No one else offered. Declan had never known people like the ones he traveled with. They rarely volunteered to help. The women maybe would, most of them anyway, but their husbands wouldn't let them. In Ireland, it was all about helping each other to survive. People always tried to make do. If one family was evicted, everyone who could took at least one family member in. Of course, that was before the Great Hunger; then it became against the law to take in others. People hardly had enough to feed themselves.

His thoughts went to Alana the woman he'd planned to marry. Her family could not afford the rent due, and all their belongings, of which there were few, were taken out of the house and the house was set on fire. He hadn't even been there. He worked every spare moment to feed his own family. There had been no tearful goodbye. Alana and her family were just gone. There hadn't been room for them in the workhouse. He'd heard later they had frozen to death. She was no more than skin and bones he was told. Waves of sadness and loneliness washed over him. No one had ever measured up to his sweet Alana.

He had his brother Heath climb into the wagon first so he could take the weight of her head and shoulders. They gently lay her on a pile of quilts. The other women must have loaned what they had. His heart softened toward them.

"I'm going to get her things."

"I'm going with you," Harrison said.

"I can do it," Declan said.

"I don't want you shot, and I don't want you hanged for strangling the man dead."

Declan nodded and gave in. Harrison was usually right.

Ebba Barnes stood alone behind the wagon with Luella's things in a gunny sack. "It ain't much. Thank you both." Tears poured down her face. "Please take good care of her and tell her, tell her… I'm not allowed to talk to her again."

"Things might seem bleak now, Ebba. Give it some time. Luella will be taken care of."

"Thank you both." She held out the bag and Declan took it from her.

When they were far enough away from the Barnes wagon Declan sighed. "How does a man do that to his daughter?"

"I have no idea," Harrison said. "Come by our fire tonight. Cora will want to be sure you are feeding Luella."

Declan stopped and stared. "Won't Cora be taking care of her?"

"Sure, for personal needs and bandaging her up, but she'll be in your wagon. Just make sure one of you is with her in case she needs something."

Relieved, Declan smiled. "We can do that. I guess we'll need to push on. I haven't forgotten there are signs of Indians being about."

"Cora found that arrowhead and we've seen many tracks. It's best we stay vigilant."

"We will."

LUELLA BIT down on her lip to keep from screaming. Mrs. Chapman sat close, but she had nodded off. The laudanum was wearing off and the pain in her leg was unbearable. Would it heal or would she have to use a crutch? Had she really been disowned? The wagon jolted in another hole in the trail. She couldn't do it anymore. She had to stop. They lurched to the left and then to the right before the wagon steadied again. Ouch, that was certainly a big rock this time.

The swaying of the wagon made her sick to her stomach. The creaking noises of the wheels were so loud. The metallic taste of the blood from her lip disgusted her. Every little thing made her miserable. The biggest hurt was her heart. It was broken. Maybe if she healed and showed her father how helpful she was, he'd want her back. By then he'd have noticed just how much of the work she did. She shouldered more than the rest and she never complained. It would all be up to her mother now, and that would just tire her out. Her mother was certainly with child again. Why wouldn't her father leave her be? The doctor had warned that another child could kill her. So many had already been born dead. Surely her father should have some compassion.

"You bit right through your lip." Mrs. Chapman pressed a wet cloth.

Luella winced and pulled away with a whimper.

"Hold still mind," admonished Mrs. Chapman, and she reapplied the cloth, holding it in place for a time and then lowering it to look at it. "There, it's stopped bleeding. Now how do you feel?"

"As though I was run over by a wagon wheel," quipped Luella. She lifted her head from the pillow and moaned as a wave of nausea struck. "And sick to my stomach."

"You seem to know what is going on," Mrs. Chapman said, staring into Luella's eyes. "I'll fill a cup with water and add a few drops of laudanum. I do have to say you have been taken in by the three most handsome men in the whole party."

"What do you mean? Am I doing something improper?"

"No, of course not," Mrs. Chapman hastened to assure her. "I didn't mean to upset you. The wagon is owned by the

Walshes. In fact, Cora will take my place soon. You are in perfectly fine and proper hands." She stirred the laudanum and water, and Luella raised her head a bit. By the time Luella finished the water she wasn't sure if she drank most or spilled it on herself. It was hard to drink while jostling around.

"We'll make ginger tea when we stop. That will help with a bad stomach. We'll be passing by Courthouse Rock soon. I'm going to pull some of this canvas up so we can see it."

It wasn't too long after that the biggest formation she'd ever seen appeared. "Why do they call it Courthouse Rock?"

"Its shape is reminiscent of the courthouse in Independence. We'll also be passing by the smaller rock which is named Jailhouse Rock. It'll be something to see, won't it? In the middle of all this emptiness, this majestic part of the earth is here. Almost as if they were sculpted here from nothing. Such sights remind me that God made the earth."

"It is astonishing," Louella mumbled. The medicine was working, but she wanted to see the Jailhouse Rock. It seemed to take forever to pass by until she saw it. She smiled. Indeed, God was the sculptor.

The next time she woke the wagon was still. The canvas was still rolled up on the sides and she had a view of a different rock. Only, it was so much bigger than a rock. She sniffed. Somewhere close by, food was cooking. They would be here for the night.

"I'm glad you were able to rest, Luella," Cora said as she climbed into the wagon. She held her arms out until Harrison put Essie in her arms. Essie fussed until she gazed at Luella. Abruptly her cries ceased, and she stared, apparently fascinated.

"She certainly likes you," Cora said. "Ginger tea is being made now. I waited until you were up so it would be fresh. Harrison will bring it. Then we'll see if you can keep any food down. Was the ride horrendous? I almost froze on this trip and had to spend a week in the back of a wagon. Not the best of memories. It's too bumpy to sew. Thankfully I has a Bible to read. I could loan you mine while you're laid up, or—"

"I have mine she can use," Declan said. He drew a sharp breath and quickly added, "I wasn't listening in! Harrison wanted to know if I should bring the tea over. He's busy trying to make the dumplings like you showed him but they aren't turning out like yours. But don't worry we'll be fine. Luella is the one we need to worry about."

Luella offered a weak smile. He made her feel warm inside with his kind manner. "I would like to borrow your Bible. What is that one called?" She pointed to one of the rock formations in the distance.

"Chimney Rock. I could have sworn over and over while I drove that we'd be near it at any time. It appears closer than it is. Captain London said we'll stop there tomorrow for two days. We're all looking forward to it." He was suddenly quiet as though he thought he talked too much. "I'll get the tea."

Luella waited for Cora to tease her about Declan but she didn't.

"Had you met Declan, Heath and Zander before?"

"Briefly, but my pa didn't allow any men near me. He was right of course. I want to get married someday and I don't want to be with anyone but my husband." She shook her head. "I see other girls sneaking away into the woods at night. I hope they are just kissing the boys."

"It sounds like you were brought up correctly." Cora turned and took the cup from Declan.

"There is more keeping warm by the fire if you need it, miss," he said, shuffling his feet. "I have guard duty tonight. I just wanted you to know that one of us will sleep under the wagon and I don't want you to hear us and be scared."

"Thank you for everything," she said and smiled again as faint warmth seeped into her face. He was rather handsome. She'd never known anyone with red hair before, and his eyes were the same light color of the sky. His accent was fascinating.

"I'm glad to help." He turned and left and she put her hands on her cheeks.

"I think I have a fever," she said.

"Here drink your tea. Just sip it and put Declan out of your mind and then your fever will go away." Cora smiled. "Declan made you blush, that's why your face heated like that."

"Oh, did I turn red? Did he see me?" She widened her eyes as her cheeks grew even warmer.

"No, it's getting dark. After you drink your tea, we'll take care of any personal needs and then get you ready for bed."

"Has my family asked after me?" She held her breath.

Compassion filled Cora's gaze. "No, sweetheart not yet."

Luella sat back and sipped her tea.

An hour later, she had her night gown on and was struggling to endure the pain. Laudanum only took the edge off. She was fine if she didn't move. Cora had washed and dressed many abrasions that Luella hadn't even realized she had. What would happen to her? Her future was blank. There no longer were any plans she could look forward to. She just hoped that she'd walk again and that she wouldn't be left to take care of herself. How old did she have to be to claim land in Oregon? So long as she healed she could do all she needed to except build the house.

She sighed. Or maybe she wouldn't even get to Oregon. The Walshes seemed to be good people, but if her own father could turn her away, what would keep anyone else from doing the same? She'd have to find a husband and fast. There were a few single men with wagons. Leo Span always smiled at her. He was about twenty years old and nice looking, but he catered to his mother an awful lot. Davis Bird traveled alone. He'd have room in his wagon. He seemed nice enough, but he never washed. Well most in the party were filthy, but they washed *once* in a while. Davis hadn't changed his clothes in two months. Someone said he was twenty-five. Who else? There was Jimmy Tomlin. He liked to watch her—and every other female. She'd seen him peeking in wagons watching women dress, but no one had believed her. A shudder rippled through her. Besides, he was too old at thirty-seven.

At eighteen she was more than old enough to marry but most of the young men were either married or didn't have their own wagon. Maybe she could get Davis Bird to take a bath. If she cleaned his wagon and washed his clothes and bedding, he might be tolerable. But how was she to get his attention?

She'd have to spend time outside of the wagon. It hurt to move but... Being left behind couldn't happen. She would never survive.

"Ma'am, it's Zander," the young man called softly from outside. "I'll be under the wagon for the first half of the night and then Declan will be here. Good night." He rolled under the wagon. She heard him moving and mumbling, probably getting the rocks out from under him, he settled down.

She stared at the canvas above her. She'd rather sleep during the day so she didn't have to feel the rough road as they traveled. Zander's nose made a whistling sound when he took a breath. It wasn't very loud, but it made her smile.

Hours later she heard Declan wake Zander, who responded none too gently, with a few grunts and a lot of movement.

"Shh, she's sleeping," Declan said.

"I know that," Zander replied defensively.

"Don't worry, I can't sleep," she said in a loud whisper.

"Was that Luella?" Zander asked.

"Who else would it be?" She could picture Declan shaking his head.

She heard a bit of rustling and then all was quiet for a long while.

"Good night, Luella," Declan said softly.

"Good night, Declan." She smiled to herself. Too bad she couldn't add any of the men who worked for Harrison to her list of possibilities. They didn't have their own wagons, so just what did they plan to do once they got to their destination? Fort Laramie wasn't supposed to be too far from Chimney Rock. Did they have places for the wives of the soldiers there? Maybe they'd pass near another wagon party and she'd catch someone's eye.

All of her thinking had dimmed her hopes. What if nothing worked? Her best plan would be to stay at the fort until she found a husband. Her thoughts kept swirling round and round until she finally heard the sounds of the camp coming awake.

Mothers scolded, children complained, and fathers threatened. Just like her family. Her heart dropped. She'd do well to remember she didn't have a family anymore.

"Are you awake?" It was Declan.

"Yes."

"Would you like some coffee before Cora can come to help you?"

"That would be very nice, thank you."

Declan loosened the cinch rope at the back of the wagon and looked in. "I'll raise the canvas again after you're dressed and all. You'll be able to look at Chimney Rock all day. The Captain said we'll stay here an extra day."

"Thank you for being so thoughtful."

He wasn't gone but a minute before he stuck his head back in. "Sorry, just found out we're leaving right now. There were at least three Indians near the camp last night. I never saw a thing. Hold on, it'll be a hard ride."

Her heart beat faster. Indians wouldn't even want her since she couldn't walk. People hurried all around her. She dipped her cup into the half-full bucket and got some water then reached for the medicine. She hastily poured some into the water and drank it down. She had just finished swallowing when the wagon lurched and she fell back.

She hoped everyone escaped, her family included.

"Do you know how to use a rifle?" Declan yelled over his shoulder.

"Yes."

"Good, we might need you to shoot."

"I don't think I'll be helpful. I took medicine and I'm feeling strange."

"How strange?" he yelled. "How much did you take?"

"I poured—"

"What?"

"I poured some I don't know how much!"

"Drops right?"

Oh no, what had she done. She didn't even think about how much to put into the water.

She held on even though she was lying down. "No! No drops!"

CHAPTER TWO

*T*he oxen were at their limit when one scout, Oscar Randolph, signaled for them to corral. The settlers quickly made a circle with their wagons and put only the livestock needed to pull their wagons in the middle so they couldn't be driven off by Indians.

Heath ran to Declan. "I'll unyoke, you'll need to move Luella. Grab the rifles and extra bullets."

Declan had already gathered the firearms. Now he went back in to get Luella, who was sleeping through it all. He'd been worried about Indians and about her dying from too much medicine. He squatted down and picked her up, covers and all. She was still wearing her nightgown.

"Heath, grab the straw tick. She's hardly dressed, and the ground might give her a chill."

They got her settled behind one of the wagon wheels. She still slept but her breathing looked to be normal.

Zander slid under the wagon and rolled to them. "I didn't see one Indian out there. I'm going to the Walsh wagon to help." He crawled out and stood, then ran off with his head ducked along the line of wagons.

Declan lay down next to Luella and looked out from under the wagon.

"I don't see anything." In fact, once everyone got settled, ready to shoot it grew eerily quiet.

Luella rolled over and put her arm over his shoulder. He was trying to figure out how to move her without causing more pain.

"You have everyone's attention," Heath murmured.

Gently he rolled her onto her back and leaned over her to adjust her covers. She mumbled something and he leaned over again and put his ear closer to the mouth.

"What did you say?" He studied her face. She was still sleeping.

"Get off her," Heath whispered harshly.

Declan furrowed his brow. What was wrong? "I thought she woke up." He glanced over his shoulder and saw too many women glaring at him. "What did I do?"

"Let's just concentrate on keeping everyone safe," Heath advised.

They both hunkered down and scanned the area. They waited and waited, and there wasn't a sign of trouble.

"Heath, who saw the moccasin, prints? Were they big or small? How many were there?"

"I'm not sure but Micky—you know the one that dresses like a man—she wears moccasins. She grew up in the mountains trapping with her Pa."

Declan groaned. "Her pa wears them too."

"I'll go see what Harrison thinks," Heath said before he raced off.

Declan kept one eye on Luella and another on the land beyond the wagon circle. What had he done wrong to have the women glaring at him? Did they think he took advantage of Luella? That was all he needed. He'd ask Zander or Heath to drive the wagon. He would not get tangled up in anything involving a woman.

His heart hurt as his thoughts drifted to Alana as they so often did. If only he could have saved her. If only he'd known where she'd had gone. Sometimes even now he felt guilty eating a heaping plateful of food. He remembered when there was nothing but cornmeal and little of it.

"Declan? What's going on?" Luella asked, her words slightly slurred.

He turned his head and smiled. "Someone claims to have seen signs of Indians in the camp and we packed up and rode hard. Now we're waiting for the Indians to arrive."

"You don't sound convinced that will happen."

"I really don't know. How are you feeling?"

"My arm hurts. I should put it in a sling."

"What about your shoulder and your leg?"

"Those hurt too but my arm is almost unbearable." She turned her head and when she turned back to him her steel-blue eyes were full of tears.

He gazed in the direction she had been looking and saw her family. Her father was scowling but her brothers were laughing.

"I'm sorry. I know your father is the last person you wanted to see."

She nodded. "Why are people staring at us? Shouldn't they be looking for the Indians?"

"If you notice it's the women staring. They think I did something to you. I'm not sure what they think I did but from their faces I think it wasn't something good."

"What happened?" Her voice was becoming stronger, and she frowned.

"I carried you out here since you were asleep from the medicine. I leaned close a couple times to make sure your quilt was covering you. Then you were mumbling and I put my ear near your mouth but I don't know what you said. Heath says it probably looked indecent from where they were watching."

"Oh my. Well you didn't do anything improper."

"You're wearing your nightgown." He didn't mention her blond hair was unbound and mussed

"My goodness why can't people mind their own business? I took too much laudanum, that's all. I don't understand people and the way they jump to conclusions. Let's not worry about it."

He nodded and stared across the grass. He knew that wouldn't be the end of it. Where was Heath?

Zander plopped down beside him. "Harrison said for you to stop talking to Luella. Don't look at her. People are talking, and it isn't good. He wants you at his wagon, and then Heath will come here."

Luella opened her mouth as if to say something, but then she snapped it closed. Declan picked up his gun, checked it, and then scurried to the Walsh wagon. Heath skedaddled as soon as Declan got there.

"I think you're right about the moccasin prints. I'm not sure if anything else was seen or not. It's best to be cautious," Harrison said.

Declan nodded.

"It's also best if you keep your distance from Luella," warned Harrison. "Best to be cautious, though people are nosey, if you ask me."

"And wrong," Cora chimed in.

"I'm not going to pay them any mind. It's my business what I do." He glanced at Cora. "Or don't do."

"Just be aware," Harrison suggested.

"I will."

They lay on the ground for another half hour before Captain London announced it was a false alarm. Then he added, "But we must remain vigilant. Everyone, let's get ready to go!" he called.

There was much grumbling. No one had eaten much that day. Thankfully, Cora had a whole pan of cornbread that they split amongst themselves. Luella claimed not to be hungry, but Cora wrapped it and put it in the wagon with her.

IT WAS a disappointment to see Zander driving instead of Declan. She mentioned rolling up the canvas to Zander, but he didn't like the idea. "Thing is, if you can see out, anyone can see in. Like Indians."

She sighed in disappointment. It would have been so nice to have a view while she bumped along. Would she ever heal enough to take care of herself? She had really fallen hard yesterday; she sure was lucky the wagon wheel hadn't killed her.

How could her father have abandoned her? Sure, she was hurt now. *But being injured is no reason to leave your daughter behind.*

Her father's glare and her brothers' laughter hurt deeply. They weren't laughing at her, true, but her circumstances didn't even impact them. Now to know people were talking about her and Declan? She'd once been one to gossip herself, but never again. How many people had she hurt with her words? Now she knew what it was like to be talked about.

She reached for Declan's Bible and opened it to a page marked by an envelope. It just had Declan's name on it and it looked like a female had written it. Was he expecting a woman to join him from Ireland? He was a handsome man, so why shouldn't he? The girl was lucky.

How would she battle the gossip? Sometimes denials

made people believe the gossip even more. But ignoring it didn't make it die down either. People only assumed there was something to hide. Crying would only show her shame. She sighed. She'd never been one to give people a second chance. Her parents were the same way. Why hadn't she realized how wrong it was?

She stared at the Bible. She needed to be truthful with herself. She knew how wrong and hurtful her actions had been. Sometimes when a person suffered she'd be glad, thinking as though that person deserved it.

Lord I thought myself as a victim having to do all the chores. I thought myself better than those who didn't have to labor all day. I hated the girls who had time to laugh and make friends. Though I never started a rumor, I was more than glad to pass it on as truth. I suppose it's only right that it should happen to me. You reap what you sow. It's hurtful and it's wrong, and please Lord, forgive me. I always thought of myself as kind and giving. I suppose I was before this trip. Back home everyone had the same lot. I thought myself stronger than others since I did so much more. Sometimes it made me bitter. I guess the bitterness spread. Please help me keep my mouth closed and not to talk about others. Is that why my parents threw me away? Am I not nice anymore?

A tear rolled down her face as she began to read. She'd heard the Bible read to her many times and was made to read it herself, but it was hard to make sense of what was being said. Why did one person quote *an eye for an eye* while another would quote *Vengeance is mine saith the Lord?*

She knew right from wrong and vowed to walk the right path. But she'd need her faith in God to do it.

Finally, hours later, they stopped. There wasn't a spot on her body that hadn't been banged. Zander hadn't even checked on her, not once.

Cora climbed into the wagon. "We need to get you dressed even though you'll need to change back in a few hours." She took a dress out of the gunny sack. "We'll put this on for now and I'll stitch up a dress that will button from top to bottom. It'll be easy to get on and off."

"You've been very kind to me, Cora."

"People helped me when I needed it. I'm just passing the kindness along."

"What a wonderful idea. I will pass on kindness too." She was going to try hard.

After she dressed, Harrison carried her out to their fire and set her down on a few folded up blankets. She faced Chimney Rock, and it was more glorious than she had imagined. It looked massive and almost the color of a rusty tool. The very top was the shape of a chimney.

"I feel so small in comparison." She smiled.

"I think most of us do," Cora replied. "I don't want to upset your meal but there has been some talk about you and Declan. We know it isn't true, and soon people will remember that you are both moral people. We considered banning Declan from the wagon but it's silly. I won't change my life around for a few old gossips."

"We've asked all three to dine with us to show that we aren't concerned," Harrison added.

Her face heated. "I've been such a bother."

"Not at all," Zander said as he sat next to her. "What do you think of the rock?"

"It's majestic."

He smiled. "I like that word, majestic."

Declan tipped his hat to both women and sat next to Zander and Heath did the same and then he took a seat next to Declan.

"Are we staying an extra day?" Luella asked, hoping the answer was yes.

"Sorry, I know you get thrown around in the back but

Captain London wants to make up for the long stop we made mid-morning," Declan said.

"I was looking forward to an extra day," Cora said with a heavy sigh. "I have diapers to wash."

Harrison's laugh was quickly subdued when Cora glared at him.

"I wish I could help you," Luella said.

"I'll help her. We'll wash them after supper and hopefully they'll dry during the night."

Cora smiled at Harrison and Luella felt a bit of envy. They were evidently in love.

"Then Sally Waverly, Emily Swatt, and Sue Bandor will stop by to sew you a dress, Luella." Cora said.

"I can probably remake something I already have."

Zander laughed. "One handed?"

"I didn't say it would look good." She smiled and the camaraderie made her heart feel lighter.

"I'm sure there is something I can do to help," Luella said after the laughter died down.

"In all honesty, I'd rather help you get ready for bed before it gets dark. It'll be easier on us both. I'm going to help you change and Mrs. Chapman will put some ointment on the abrasions you didn't mention yesterday."

Luella's face heated. "I needed so much tending I didn't want to be a bother. But now, realizing my folly, I would like them looked at." She gazed past her companions and wasn't surprised to see all the stares. "I don't suppose my parents have asked after me?"

Harrison cleared his throat. "That just may take a little time. Your father has a wide stubborn streak. Don't you worry, we are here to take care of you and you're welcome to come to Oregon with us."

"Th-thank you." Her eyes moistened. God was with her and had given her a path to follow.

"Well since you're family…" Zander stood and then bent to scoop her up. "I think it's fine if I carry you—or Heath or Declan. We're trying to survive out here, not put on a society party."

Declan laughed. "Society party?"

"You know all those rules bowing and kissing a lady's hands and standing up when a lady stands."

"You mean the rules of society. Those are rules of people in England. I think the manners your poor mother had to beat into your head will be just fine here." Declan's smile widened.

"My mother was a saint. We will have no more talk about the sainted woman. Come along Luella."

She couldn't help the laughter that bubbled out of her. "I go where you go. You're carrying me."

Zander didn't say a word he just started off to the wagon. "Heath and I will be around just as much as Declan so no one can say you're acting improper with Declan."

"Just all three of you?"

"You don't have to look for flaws in my plans. They tend to come out on their own." He nodded to Sally and Rod Waverly. "Don't smile or laugh or talk. People will talk."

"Am I allowed to breathe?"

"If you'd be quiet, you wouldn't need to breathe as often." His boyish grin was too much, and she laughed loud and hard. She laughed even harder at his grumbling as he set her in the wagon.

"Cora will be here to do anything you need. We wouldn't want to tarnish my reputation any." He yelled it, and she expected the whole party heard him.

She'd never thought to use humor to dispel rumors.

CHAPTER THREE

*E*very day must seem like the one before to Luella. Sitting inside the wagon, riding the rutted and bumpy trail, nothing to do but read his Bible or stare at the land they passed. Declan wished there was something he could do for her or with her to brighten her day. She was healing nicely, and she hoped to walk by the time they got to Fort Laramie.

Sally Waverly, Emily Swatt, Sue Bandor and Cora sewed Luella a dress in record time. It was an ugly gray dress with black buttons all down the front. Frankly, he hated it but it was practical he supposed.

He tried to avoid the bumps, but it was a useless job; many trains had passed before them, and the ruts were all over the road. She was cheerful and never complained, though. She had stopped asking about her family over a week ago. He often saw her gazing at her brothers with sadness in her eyes, but they never seemed to notice. Many people had talked to her father to no avail. He refused to listen to anyone including the captain and the preacher.

If anyone had asked him, he would have told them that

her father was a fool. Luella was delightful and smart. Declan enjoyed their conversations. It was as though she could never express her opinion before, and knowing her father, it was probably forbidden. She had been quiet at first but after learning what she had to say mattered, she kept talking.

It was a bit like watching a flower bloom. She had him entranced, but he stepped away often. He needed to honor Alana's memory. He saw the questions in her eyes when he withdrew but he didn't want to talk about it.

"I'm going to walk today," she shouted from inside the wagon.

"It's probably not a good idea."

"Declan, I know you mean well, but my health and soundness has nothing to do with you. I've offered my friendship, and you've spurned it many times. My feelings can't take much more so I'll let you be."

He didn't know what to say, so he said nothing. He didn't blame her, yet he would give anything if he could make her his own. It just wasn't possible. But he couldn't stay away either. Being near her was like basking in the most illuminating glow. Walking away was like walking into a dark chasm. Zander teased him about it, while Heath fretted over it.

Truth was, he had nothing to offer her. He didn't even own a wagon. He was just a poor Irishman trying to make a new life for himself. What did his future hold? He and Zander and Heath planned to get land and build a ranch. If that didn't work out, they knew how to farm too. Or maybe they would end up doing both. This land was certainly different from Ireland, and once they claimed their free land, they wouldn't have rents to pay. No one would throw their things out into the road and burn down their homes. There were those in the world with no mercy. Some English landholders had learned that more money could be paid if they raised cattle on the land instead of having tenants. Too often the landholders had waited until there was no food or money to be had before turning their tenants out. He relaxed his hands that had balled into fists as he thought about all the injustice. God would deal with them and their greed. Of that Declan was certain. He shuddered, remembering people crying out to God before they dropped dead while building government funded roads. They were skeletons paid a mere pittance, not nearly enough for them to afford to feed their families.

No, it would be too disloyal to Alana to keep basking in Luella's glow.

The wagons ahead began circling for the night, and he followed them into the formation. Tomorrow around midday they were supposed to be at Fort Laramie. Maybe they'd get an extra day to rest. He could always spend time with Harrison's horses.

Declan put on the brake and wrapped the lines around it. He went to the back and Luella already had the tailgate down. He went to swing her up in his arms but she stepped back.

"You'll set me on my feet?"

He wasn't happy about it, but he nodded. Carefully, he lifted and set her down right in front of him. He wanted to groan at the way she looked up at him. It was as if she was inviting him to kiss her. He could see she cared for him. Moving back, he held out his hands for her to take. Then he retreated another step and watched her take a step forward. The happiness on her face was too much. He ground his teeth. It was all too much.

"Heath, would you mind stepping in for me? I have something I need to take care of."

Heath took Luella's hands. "You're doing really well."

Declan kept walking until he found a spot to be alone.

How was he going to make it to Oregon without going mad? Maybe now that she could walk, her parents would want her back. But he shook his head. He didn't want that for her. He wanted her to be safe and happy. It just could never happen with him. Maybe he just needed time and distance from her.

THAT WAS the last time she would allow him to hurt her. She had her pride, and she should have given up weeks ago. The problem was she loved him. He felt a connection to her she knew he did. Her heart ached worse now than it had when her parents rejected her. Her future didn't worry her any longer, now that the Walshes had said she was welcome to live with them. But what about Declan? Would she ever learn to not love him? There wasn't anything she could do about it, but that didn't stop her heart from speeding up whenever he was near, didn't stop that fluttering in her stomach when he glanced her way.

"Look at you walking!" Cora exclaimed. "That's wonderful."

Luella gave her a ghost of a smile. "Thank you."

Heath shuffled his feet. "I'd best see to the oxen." And with that, he settled Luella's hands on the wagon so she could steady herself and then walked off.

Cora waited until it was just the two of them and Essie before she spoke again. "What's wrong? You look as though you've just lost your best friend."

"An interesting way to put it."

Cora covered her mouth with her hand. "It's Declan, isn't it?"

Luella stared at the ground in silence.

"I'm so sorry," murmured Cora.

The realization that Cora had noticed her feelings for

Declan was disturbing, and Luella started to feel unsteady so she sat on a crate Heath had set beside the wagon. "I know there have been times when he's avoided me, but I figured we'd be together in the end."

"It's not the end yet."

"He's walked away from me for the last time. My heart can't take much more. Why couldn't I have fallen for Heath or Zander?" She didn't wait for Cora to answer before she shook her head. "I'll be fine. It's just going to take some time, I suppose."

"We're having a dance tomorrow night at the fort. A change will do you good."

"Yes, I think it will." She smiled for Cora's sake. But that smile faded as the night went on. Declan didn't have dinner with them. Zander told her Declan volunteered for double guard duty. As soon as she helped with the dishes she, begged off, declaring she was exhausted.

Heath walked her to the wagon and helped her in.

"He's a fool, you know," Heath said.

"I know, and so am I." Did everyone know? Her throat went dry as sand. "Good night."

Sleep didn't come easy. A little while into the night, she heard someone outside the wagon. She thought it was Zander waking Heath up for guard duty until a shot rang out.

She wanted to run, but she stayed still and listened.

Sounds of a scuffle reached her, and then Heath yelled, "I got him. See if he brought any friends."

"Where is Luella? Where is she?" It was Declan.

"Look in the wagon. She's fine, I expect."

"You expect?" Declan opened the canvas in the back and jumped right into the wagon. He looked like a mighty warrior frantically glancing around.

"I'm here." She crawled out behind a trunk. "What happened? Was anyone hurt?"

Declan took her into his arms and held her tight. He didn't say anything for a while. Then he let go and sat back. "Heath got him. The tracks lead right to the back of the wagon."

"Him who?"

"An Indian. Maybe he's the one that's been watching us. I've felt it more than a few times, a tingling on the back of my neck. I knew someone was watching the group. Stay here while we look around." He climbed out.

Harrison stood at the end. "Wrap that quilt around you. You're staying in the wagon with Cora and Essie for the rest of the night."

She wrapped herself and before she knew it she was being carried by Harrison. What would the gossips have to say about this?

"I got her. You ladies stay put so I know you're safe."

"We will," Cora assured him.

Luella climbed into the back.

"Was it scary?" asked Cora

Luella shook her head. "I didn't even know what was happening until they got him. Declan thinks the Indian has been following the train for a while?"

"He mentioned it a time or two," admitted Cora. "He told us to be careful because he was sure someone was watching the train. I didn't think much of it. Those prints found were from people in our own party. I found an arrowhead but learned that Ash Hollow was once a place where Indians lived. Strange. How many were there?"

"Only the one and he was outside my wagon."

"Oh, my. I'm glad we'll be at the fort tomorrow," Cora said as she shuddered.

"If they think they can sneak into camp and steal our

women they are mistaken!" The women stared at each other when they heard the angry words.

"Steal?" A lightheaded sensation assaulted Luella as she felt the blood drain from her face. "I think I need to lie down."

Cora moved over. "Here lie next to me. He must have seen you and took a liking to you. We'd best wait to find out the truth before we get ourselves too upset. I could come up with a couple dozen stories but none are probably what really happened."

Luella tried to put it all out of her mind, though a chill rippled through her at the thought of an Indian taking a liking to her. She glanced over at Cora's baby. "Essie is getting so big."

Cora smiled proudly. "She sure is, and she's got Harrison wrapped around her little finger. I'm blessed to have both Harrison and Essie. Sometimes you think you're headed one way and God opens another path and gives you a nudge in the right direction."

"You're happy."

"Yes, I am." Cora's eyes lit. "I'll tell you a secret. I think I'm carrying another baby. I haven't told Harrison, so please don't say anything. I want to be sure before he starts hovering over me and asking after my well-being at all times. But I felt like I was going to just burst if I didn't tell anyone. I'm so glad we're friends."

"I'm so excited for you. There is such a sparkle in your eyes. I hope you are."

"Me too."

"Luella, get out here at once!" a man's voice bellowed.

"That's my father," Luella whispered.

"Don't make me come in there!" he shouted.

Cora went to the back of the wagon. "I have a sleeping baby in here. I insist you leave!"

Luella watched in horror as her father reached in and pulled Cora out of the wagon. Swallowing hard, she crawled to the back and climbed out. Her body was beginning to hurt from all the activity. "Leave Cora alone, Pa."

Her father slapped her across the face. "That—that Indian said you invited him to come take you! How dare you endanger the rest of us with your foolish girlish ideas?"

Cora stepped forward, but Luella held up a hand to stop her.

"Cora, make sure Essie isn't scared. I'll be fine."

Luella and Cora shared a look; they both knew it was anything but fine. Cora nodded and climbed back into the wagon.

"Where did you meet him? Start talking girl!" He raised his arm to slap her again.

Out of nowhere Declan appeared and grabbed her father's arm. "We don't hit women," he said in a low warning voice.

"She's mine, and I'll do what I like. Until she weds, she belongs to me." Her father's smile bordered on evil.

Declan stood in front of her. "She is a free woman in a free land."

"No, you've got that wrong," her father corrected. "*You* are a free man in a free country. She is my daughter, which by law makes her mine. Now I suggest you get out of my way and let me have her."

"So if she belongs to you, when she weds she belongs to her husband?"

Auggie Barnes puffed out his chest. "Yes, it's finally getting through your thick Irish head."

"Well, we're getting married so you see you have no standing here."

"Just the person I was looking for," Captain London said,

eyeing the two men. "Luella, after you are dressed I will require your presence."

Harrison stepped up and swung her up into his arms. It happened so fast she screamed.

"Let's get you to your wagon. You can get dressed and then answer the captain's questions. I'll wait outside to make sure you're not disturbed." He took long strides toward the wagon she'd been riding in. "You're shaking," he murmured.

"I didn't do anything wrong."

"I know that, but the Indian says you asked him to be your husband so you could escape your family."

"For heaven's sake. Why would I do that?"

"You wouldn't." He deposited her inside the wagon. "Don't take too long. People are getting anxious."

She hurried and slipped into one of her two clean dresses, put her hair up, and picked up Declan's Bible. She stood at the back of the wagon, shocked by the number of people standing there. Declan stepped forward and helped her down. He offered her his arm. She curled her arm through and held on to him. The sun was rising but today it didn't give her much hope.

"You'll be just fine," he whispered.

She didn't believe him so she said nothing.

They had set up a rather large tent next to the captain's wagon. Declan escorted her to the entrance and opened the flap for her. Then he let her go.

Captain London sat on a crate that was higher than the crates her and the Indian were to sit on. The Scout, Simps, stood behind the Indian who had his hands tied behind him and his feet tied so he couldn't walk.

"Have a seat, Luella," Captain London said. He waited until she was seated before he sat. The higher crate gave the illusion that he was more important.

There was another crate that sat empty.

"This is how this is going to work. I will tell you what the claims are, and then you both can call two witnesses if you have them."

She stole a glance at the Indian. She half expected him to be bare-chested, but he was all dressed in buckskins. She didn't see malice in his eyes.

"Does he understand us?" she asked.

"Yes," the Indian answered for himself.

"Listen carefully. You, Luella, are charged with inviting this Indian to our camp so he could take you away. You promised to be his wife." He tilted his head toward the Indian. "I charge him with sneaking into our camp with dangerous weapons."

"My charges sound worse than his," she objected.

"Name your first witness."

"I go first?" Hopefully that would be in her favor. "Very well, Cora please."

The captain asked Cora a few things but his last question had Luella paying close attention.

"Cora do you have any information about Luella's plans for her future? Has she ever named a man she'd like to marry?"

"We, Harrison and I, have offered her a home with us. There is a young man she likes, but they are just getting to know each other."

"Who is this man?"

Cora hesitated, her gaze darting toward Luella, almost in apology. "It's Declan," she answered.

"Thank you, Cora, you may leave and please don't repeat what was said in here."

Heat licked at Luella's cheeks. Why would Cora tell the captain her private thoughts?

"Luella, I will call in Declan as your other witness."

What type of proceeding was this? She waited in dread.

34

Declan walked through the flap. He didn't even glance at her. He probably thought *she* had called on him to be her witness.

"Declan, there were rumors about you and Luella for a while. Was there any truth to them?"

"No, it was just gossip. I wouldn't show disrespect toward her that way."

"It's been said that if she could marry anyone, it would be you. What do you have to say to that?"

Declan met her gaze, his expression seemed set in stone. "We are like-minded."

"So you plan to marry Luella?"

"It has crossed my mind, yes."

"Thank you, Declan."

He didn't glance at her when he left.

Next came her father.

"Auggie Barnes, you have said that your daughter asked the Indian to take her away."

"Yes, I did and it's the truth. She's always been a bad seed."

"Is that bruise on her face from you?"

"Yes it is, and there is more coming for her."

"Mr. Eagle's Nest—"

"Captain London, I don't think that's his name," the scout said.

"Are you sure?"

The Indian stood. "He's sure. I want my pelts and silver bracelets back and I will not be bringing that man any horses." He pointed at Auggie. "I don't want any part of this game you play. She never asked to be my wife. I can tell." He sat back down.

"Luella, you may leave."

"Now see here!" her father yelled.

She stood straight and tall and walked across the tent to the tied man. "I am very sorry for what my father did. I have never seen you before, and I'm sorry he lied. You don't deserve to be tied up, and I hope you go on and find a wonderful wife."

Something flickered in his eyes as he studied her for a long moment. When he spoke, his words sent a wave of shock through her. "You are an honorable woman."

Luella walked out of the tent. She didn't know where to go or who to look for. The whole party was there staring at her and saying hurtful things. She turned and ran in the opposite direction. She found a boulder to sit behind as she cried. She was not a loose or fallen woman. She wasn't unfit to marry. This wasn't her fault. But they thought it all to be true. Her father had done something much crueler than throwing her away; he had sold her to an Indian. The Indian had honor, but her father probably didn't know it or care.

But Declan had lied for her and humiliation swept through her. There would never be enough time for them to get to know each other or for his heart to heal. She'd just hide in the wagon the rest of the trip and keep to herself. Her leg hurt so much anyway.

She leaned back against the big rock and studied the blue sky. Big, white, puffy clouds sailed past, pushed by the wind. A nice breeze teased her cheeks, and it didn't seem as hot for a change. She sighed. Her only crime was jumping out of the wagon while it was moving. Plenty of people did it but they hadn't been hurt. But the rage her father had shown—had he always hated her? He was never nice, but he hadn't been this cruel before.

She supposed she wasn't good enough to be anyone's wife. Maybe once she got to Oregon and found a place where no one knew her, she'd make a whole new life and people would like her. She drew in a shaky breath. She needed to calm herself. The captain probably wanted to get on with their journey. He'd cancel their extra day at the fort, and it would be her fault.

"Luella?" Zander's soft call startled her.

"I'm here behind the boulder," she answered.

"We'll be pulling out soon. I was sent to get you." He shuffled his feet and didn't quite meet her gaze. He looked so uncomfortable being alone with her.

She stood and used the rock to get her balance then started walking back to the wagons. She didn't say a word or ask what happened. It would be best to allow Zander to go his own way.

She didn't have to pass many people before she got to her wagon. Zander hadn't followed her. She would have to climb up herself. Maybe if she climbed up to the bench in the front using the wheel as leverage she could then get over the bench to the back. But just thinking about it was exhausting. She didn't want to wait for whoever was driving to help her, and she didn't see a clear way to get in herself. She stared into the back for a moment longer before she turned.

"We need to talk," Declan said softly.

Luella jumped, startled. When had he come up to the wagon? "I'm so sorry. I'm not the one who called you as my witness. I wouldn't have involved you in my troubles. I'm rather embarrassed about the whole thing." She couldn't look at his face, so she stared at a button on his shirt instead.

He put his hand under her chin and lifted her head until she was looking at him. Then he cupped the side of her cheek that was bruised. "He will never hurt you again."

"Did they make him leave?" Her heart beat faster as it usually did when Declan was near.

"No, nothing like that. The Indian left. He seemed to admire you and told us that he would bring no one back to exact revenge for your father's actions. He took back his pelts and things he had used to pay for you."

"I'm glad they let him go. He really thought my father had the right to sell me." Her eyes welled up. "I'm sorry. I'm trying not to cry. Could you just give me a boost into the wagon or ask someone else?"

He stroked her cheek with the back of his hand. "Your father wants you in his wagon."

She froze in place. Her mind refused to comprehend what Declan had just said. It was hard to breathe, and she started to fall.

Declan caught her and laid her on the ground. "Heath, I need your help!"

Heath left the oxen and came running. "Oh, boy. I'll get Cora."

"Carry her to my wagon," her father insisted.

Her father's voice drew her out of her stupor and she struggled to sit up. "I can walk." She got onto her hands and knees and suddenly she was in Declan's arms. "Thank you." She stood on her feet and stepped away. "Thank both of you for all you've done." She turned and took a step.

"You're *not* going back to his wagon," Declan declared.

"I say she does."

"I think I can take care of this." Minister Paul stepped in front of her. "I'm here to marry Declan to Luella."

Her jaw dropped, and before she could protest, Cora and Harrison joined them along with Captain London.

"I'm not giving her away."

"Maybe not this time," Captain London said. He smiled down at Luella. "It would honor me to do it."

Before she knew what was happening, she was married to Declan Leary. As she stood staring at her new husband, he kissed her lips lightly.

"Let's get ready to go!" Captain London said. "If we move fast enough, we'll be able to spend the night dancing and celebrating.

Everyone scurried. Declan lifted her to the front bench and then he helped Heath with the oxen. After that he jumped up and sat beside her. He took the lines, let off the brake, and yelled "haw."

She'd never ridden in the front before. It wasn't comfortable either, but she couldn't walk, not for a bit at least. She waited for Declan to say something, but he didn't say a thing for miles. It took a toll on her nerves.

Finally she had to break the awful silence. "I never—I didn't— I'm so sorry. I know you want nothing to do with me, and I don't blame you and you were made to marry me, and that is horrible for you. You should be able to marry who you want. Marriage shouldn't be just because everyone knows my father will beat me if he gets me to his wagon. That's not fair to you. I will give you your freedom as soon as we're done with this doomed journey."

"What does that mean? Give me my freedom?" He kept his gaze straight ahead.

"If we never, well if we never have relations we can get the marriage annulled or something."

DIDN'T she take the vows they spoke in front of God seriously? It wasn't a priest that preformed the marriage but it was a man who represented God. He decided not to say anything. He wasn't ready for them to have relations anyway. He needed to finish mourning Alana first. He did enjoy Luella's company; she was witty and smart. She was a fair lass, to be sure, and very pleasing.

For better or worse, they were now one. A frown pinched his brow. Where was he supposed to sleep? If he slept elsewhere, she might get the idea that was the way it would always be, and he didn't want that. If he slept next to her, she might be scared. He sighed. He would just talk to her later, try to see what she thought. She was worried about the same thing. He wished there had been time for a veil and flowers and a ring. Many could not afford a dress, but in some families they handed the veil down.

He'd make the best of it and God willing they would be blessed with children. He didn't trust her father, so he still needed Zander and Heath to help keep watch on her. Her father might sell her to one of the soldiers at the fort. It had taken all his control to keep from hitting that man. He deserved respect as her father, but there must be exceptions.

Was Alana looking down from heaven, upset with him? He'd promised her forever, but she was dead. In his heart, her death didn't change his promise. Poor Luella deserved so much more than he could give her. She was not getting an annulment, though, for he'd promised before the Lord to take care of her, but he wasn't going to say a word until the time came.

Indians were camped out on the side of the trail trying to sell beaded moccasins, silver bracelets and items other pioneers must have left behind. Luella grabbed his arm and didn't let go. He patted her hand quickly not wanting to hold the lines in just one hand with so many people around. He needed to have complete control over the animals.

"They must be friendly or they wouldn't be allowed to stay so close to the fort. Look, there are other wagons here. It'll be nice to see a few new faces."

"Are we going to the dance tonight?" she asked almost timidly.

He glanced at her quickly. "I don't see why not? We're celebrating our wedding."

I don't know how... But she didn't know how to tell him, so instead she said, "I'm Mrs. Leary now."

"Yes you are. What a lucky lass."

"I am. I'm very lucky." She scooted closer to him. "Are you sure about the Indians? They don't look friendly."

"Did you expect them to smile at you?"

"Yes, if they want to sell their things they should smile."

"A few of the women are smiling. The young pretty ones are."

She stiffened against him. "You think they're pretty?"

"Sure they aren't as fair of face as you, but they are pretty."

She was quiet for a bit, and he knew she probably wasn't thinking anything good. "Was there something you wanted to ask me?"

"Would you—I mean if there was another woman, would you?" Her face reddened.

"I'll not be stepping out on you if that's what you're asking."

She nodded.

"I'll be asking the same of you."

Her jaw dropped. "Women don't—"

He chuckled. "They most certainly do, and it does nothing but bring shame to all involved. It breaks families involved and somehow the woman is blamed more than the man."

"I didn't know. Declan, there are many things I don't know about. I can do all the work necessary plus much more. I've had to do most of the chores on our farm." She worried at her lower lip with her teeth. "I... don't know how to act like a wife. My mother always seemed miserable, yet Cora is very happy. My mother has lost many children—they go to God before they are born, and my father blames her, and I'm afraid she's with child again." Tears welled in her eyes. Tears Declan longed to wipe away, yet he found it hard to move. "Do I stand next to you at meetings? Will we be having meals at our wagon for us, Heath, and Zander? I know to wash your clothes, but do I wash theirs too?" She frowned and added quickly, "I don't mind. Do I still sleep in the wagon, or will we have a tent? I need my father to believe the marriage is real. Do I wait until you want to go to bed or if I'm tired can I turn in earlier? My father forbade my mother to go to bed until he was ready. Harrison suggests Cora turn in when she's tired. I know we have food supplies under the second floor in the wagon. Is that for us to use or do we ask Harrison? What do I do when someone else is driving? Do I walk instead of thinking about sitting next to a man who isn't my husband?"

Stunned by the barrage, Declan managed to hold up a hand, stopping her. "Whoa! Luella you're stressing me with all your questions. You must be nervous, and you don't have to be. You do what you want. Many of the questions you have we can answer as they come up. You don't have to do anything you don't want to do, and I won't demand things of you. How does that sound?"

"Good but what do married couples do in Ireland?"

The pain in his heart sharpened. "My mother did her work, my Pa did his, but they helped each other. My mother never argued, she let my father think his word was law but my ma really held the purse strings. It worked for them." He wanted to touch her, to lay a hand on her arm in reassurance, but he settled for gentling his tone. "We'll find our way."

She smiled and nodded. "Look, there's the fort. I thought it would be much bigger."

"It's big enough, I suspect. It's not meant for the wagons to go inside the walls."

"People are going to restock?"

"I would imagine they would. I'll have to ask Harrison what he wants me to get for him."

CHAPTER FOUR

A pang of jealousy hit Luella as she watched many of the travelers walk to Fort Laramie, but she didn't have a cent to buy anything with, so there was no point to her making the journey.

Zander wasn't happy because they picked him to stay behind with some others to guard the camp. He sat on a crate near the wagon carving a piece of wood into randomly shaped splinters that fell at his feet. Things had grown tense between him and Luella since her wedding to Declan.

She took her other clean dress out of the sack and examined it, scowling at the wrinkles. She could try to iron it, but using an iron heated by the fire might not be safe. She hung it from one of the wagon ribs that the canvas was pulled over. Then she took a wet cloth and went down the length of the dress with it, hoping the wrinkles would come out as it dried. It was her Sunday best, but some probably would consider the dress ready for the rag bin.

She took the time to wash her hair and build a fire to dry it. Declan had never answered whether she was to cook, but she enjoyed cooking, so it was a task she wanted to do. A wisp of sadness touched her heart. She had offered him an annulment, best she remembered that.

She braided her hair and let it fall down her back. Coffee came next; coffee was always a good idea, especially since she couldn't just sit still. Sitting around just wasn't for her. She noticed that Zander didn't glance her way once. Was he upset for his friend? Did everyone feel bad for Declan?

She glanced at some nearby wagons. Her mother was already washing clothes. Pa wouldn't allow her to go into Fort Laramie. Luella couldn't remember the last time her mother had to wash the clothes—that had been one of Luella's chores. Since she had been kicked out of her parents' wagon, they'd passed each other once in a while, but her mother never acknowledged her. At first she thought her mother was afraid to go against her pa but every once in a while she'd look around and see her mother glaring at her.

She'd been a good daughter and couldn't understand any of it. Much of her sleep had been lost trying to figure it all out.

After pouring herself a cup of coffee, she sat down and enjoyed the almost cool breeze. The sun would set in about two hours. Would people really dance? Declan had said they would dance to celebrate their wedding. If only she knew even a few dance steps.

She heard singing in the distance and knew that Heath and Declan were almost back. Heath had his purchases with him. Declan went to the front of the wagon for a bit and then came back with a new bridle and some cloth.

He smiled as he sat and she handed him a cup of coffee.

"Tell me everything! What did they sell? Were there more Indians in the fort? What about the soldiers? Were there women that lived there?"

Heath laughed. "I didn't know you were the curious type."

Declan chuckled. "Where have you been? Luella always has lots of questions."

Confused, she didn't know what to say or if she should smile. Was he teasing? Or had she just been insulted? She sipped her coffee and stared into the fire. Declan was right, though. She did ask questions. Did he think her a pest?

Zander came over and poured himself some coffee. "How is this supposed to work? Do we cook our own meals or will Luella have to do it? Did Harrison say anything about her duties?"

Luella stood, poured out her coffee and put the cup on the tailgate. Then she walked away. *Her duties?* She didn't mind doing it, but not because it was assigned to her. She didn't work for Harrison or Zander. She was sitting right there and Zander hadn't even asked *her* about it.

It had already been a very trying day. Sold to an Indian and then married to Declan. Now she was supposed to go to a dance when she'd never been to one before. She stared out at the Platte River. At least the water would be good for the next few days.

Maybe she'd go back, put up the tent and hide in it. No one would bother her in a tent would they? She'd spent so much time inside the wagon she knew where the tent was. Then again, maybe she didn't have cause to be upset. A woman first belonged to her father and then her husband. She was freer than many but not as free as some.

Cora walked up and stood next to her with Essie in her arms. "Long day. My goodness, we did an awful lot this day, and we still have to celebrate." She leaned close and peered into Luella's eyes. "Wool gathering?"

"Yes, I just don't know where I fit." She released a sigh. "The wagon wasn't intended for me. It belongs to Harrison. I know you've been doing all the cooking since I was confined to the wagon. If you like I can cook for us all."

"I'll take you up on that soon enough," Cora answered with a smile.

Luella turned and gathered both Cora and Essie to her in one hug. "So you are sure? Congratulations. Did you tell Harrison?"

"Yes, and he's so happy. But I thought you might want to cook for your husband. It's something I like to do for Harrison. But you are under no obligation to cook for Zander and Heath. Your duties, honestly."

Heat flowed into Luella's cheeks. "So you heard that...?"

Cora nodded. "You can decide with Declan what you do on this journey. And you and I can share some tasks. But I'll cook tonight since it's your wedding day."

"I don't know what I'd do without you, Cora."

"I had a lot to learn when I got married too. It's difficult, and Zander and Heath might not make it any easier. Don't you let them treat you like some hired girl. You are Declan's wife and deserve respect. Now go get ready for the party, and we'll eat soon."

Luella nodded. She couldn't bring herself to speak. She watched Cora walk to Harrison, sighed as he kissed her cheek.

"Got kicked out so soon?" her father taunted from the back of his wagon.

Luella pretended to ignore him and walked back to her wagon. She was so exhausted, but she needed to get dressed. No one was at the wagon when she got there, which surprised her. She climbed into the back to get her dress and found a new dress hanging in its place. It was grass green trimmed in a much darker green ribbon. Inhaling in awe, she touched it with the tips of her fingers. There were stockings and shoes too, set beneath the dress. Declan must have left them as gifts. He was so generous. But how? Why? She knew he needed his money for the ranch he wanted to start with

Heath and Zander. Maybe if she didn't wear it, he could return it for the money he would need. She picked up her own dress and put it on. In no time, she upswept her hair into a bun with little tendrils framing her face. Then she went to the end of the wagon, hoping someone would be nearby to help her down.

There was Declan in a clean shirt—and he was freshly shaved! He smiled with his whole face, from the wide sweep of his mouth to his twinkling eyes. But then his smile faded. "You didn't like the dress I picked out? I knew I should have gotten the blue one but…"

"It's the prettiest dress I've ever seen. But I don't want you to spend your money on me. You'll need every bit for your ranch. I do appreciate your surprise, though, it made my heart smile."

He lifted her down and kept his hands on her waist. "You really don't care about new dresses and such?"

"Not when you have a future to build. You have your dream, and that will be expensive. The land will be free but you need to build a house and a barn. If you decide to plant a crop, you'll need a plow and livestock. I'll not take that from you for a dress. Do you think you can get your money back?"

He gave her a quick kiss on the lips and stepped back. "I've never known anyone like you except my mother. She always sacrificed so Heath and I could have what we needed." He looked deep into her eyes. "I want you to have the dress if you want it."

"I think that's the nicest thing anyone ever said, comparing me to your mother. Let's get to Cora and Harrison's."

He reached for her hand and held it as they walked to the other wagon.

HE'D SPENT time with her but there was a lot he didn't know about her. Imagine a woman turning down a becoming new dress. She was right about the money, and the dress had come dear, but she deserved to feel pretty. He smiled as she finished helping Cora with the dishes. Then they walked toward the lively music. The sound of laughter heartened him. They'd all had to be serious for too long now.

Harrison led Cora out to the where others danced. They fit well together.

Zander ran over and bumped Declan's shoulder purposely setting him a bit off balance. "Come on! Jackson got himself enough whiskey to make the lot of us giddy."

"I can't."

"Oh that's right they made you to get married today. Well, enjoy standing here and watching." With that, Zander continued on his way.

"Don't pay him any mind."

She gave him the quickest of smiles. He took her hand and led her outside fringe of the firelight.

"I have something for you, and this time you'll not refuse it. I'm not telling, mind, I'm asking. It took me a bit of time picking it out and I'm proud that I'm able to give this to you." He pulled the gold ring from his pocket. "I know we didn't plan to get married, but I believe in making the best of things. Lord only knows why he put us on this path together." He slid the ring on her finger. "I promise to be faithful and to provide for you. I promise to value your opinion and be there for you."

She stared at the ring then touched it as if she couldn't believe it was real. Her eyes shimmered. "This is beautiful. Thank you, Declan for the ring and for your kindness. I promise to help you in any way I can. I promise to be your friend and I promise to let you go when you say it's time. We'll get through this journey together, and we have the help of our friends and your brother. I believe in you. You are a man of honor and integrity, and I think I'll enjoy our short marriage."

He took her into his arms and kissed her longer. He could tell that she felt something for him. He smiled against her lips. She promised to go when *he* said it was time. He never planned to say it was time. They stood there in each other's arms and there was a rightness to them being together. "I'm glad you didn't go with Eagle Nest."

She pushed him away. "That is not his name, you know, and he is a very honorable man. My father played him for a fool, and I don't think it'll be something Swift Eagle will forget."

"His name is Swift Eagle?"

"I'm sure it's not Nest. I hope he finds a wife he loves."

As they walked back to the festivities, her father blocked their path. "I lost a lot of money today. I had to give back all those pelts and some silver. You were the payment for those things. He thought he was getting something so special and I knew I would be rich." He kicked the dirt between them. "You have disappointed me at every turn."

"I'd appreciate it if you didn't talk to my wife... ever."

His harsh laughter cut the air between them. "Good luck to you. She's a curse." And then he strode away.

Luella pretended to smile as so many people stared at them.

"He's out of your life. You won't have to worry about him. Like a sore loser he had to get his last word in." Declan tugged at her hand. "Dance with me."

"I don't know how," she whispered. "I didn't know how to tell you earlier."

His smile crinkled his eyes. "Just follow me."

He slid one hand around her waist and took her right hand in his left. He moved slowly, but he seemed to know what he was doing. She felt like a bride at that moment. Women saw her ring and smiled at her. She was one of them now, she supposed. A married woman.

Her heart beat faster as Declan pulled her a bit closer. She could smell the soap he'd used and a bit of leather. It would be so nice to lean her head on his chest, but of course, it wouldn't be proper.

Zander pulled her out of Declan's arms and wrapped both arms around her. The whiskey on his breath nauseated her. He pulled her too close, and he wouldn't let go.

"Zander, please let go. You're hurting me." Not wanting to draw more attention or upset her new husband, she tried to be as discreet as possible.

In short order, Declan squeezed Zander's shoulder and pulled him away. Much to Luella's relief, he did it in such a way no one even gave them a second look.

She accepted Declan's hand when he offered it and allowed him to lead her away from the dancing. He brought her to a table that had water with sliced lemons in it. There wasn't enough for lemonade she supposed. But it was refreshing.

"Most of the party is here," she said.

"They sure are. I'm sorry about Zander."

"He'd been drinking. I'm just glad he didn't cause a scene."

"He's had a hard life and ended up in an orphanage for a while. Not a good place to be. Then he had to be creative in finding food since there weren't any jobs. He was probably lucky he wasn't put in prison. But he's a good fella."

She smiled and nodded. Usually Zander wasn't so bad, but lately he had been showing a bit of a sullen nature.

"You look tired," Declan commented.

"Well, the day started out on a very trying note, though it's ended up nice." She sighed as weariness overtook her. "But yes, I'm tired."

"I probably should have put up the tent for us. I didn't think of it. We'll have to sleep in the wagon tonight."

"Together?"

"I think it best. I don't want your father to doubt our marriage."

"But you said..."

He took the empty cup from her and put it on the table with his. Then he held her hand and kissed the back of it. "I keep my word. We need to think of how things look to the rest, though. A man doesn't sleep under the wagon on his wedding night. It'll be cramped, but I think we can do it. I'll remember to set up the tent tomorrow for us."

They began to walk through the darkness. "Us?"

"The tent is plenty big enough for us both without having to sleep on top of each other." He chuckled, a happy sound that warmed her heart. "When Heath and I were kids, we had two more brothers and we all shared a bed. It was no bigger than the straw tick in the wagon. We were the lucky ones my poor sister had to sleep on a blanket on the floor. We'll be just fine. I promise."

She nodded. He was trustworthy, plus he didn't feel that way about her. He probably thought of her more like a sister... or maybe not. No, a man would never kiss a sister. Maybe a neighbor or a close friend, but not a woman he loved. But he would keep her safe and act like a gentleman.

They walked to the wagon. "I'll bank the fire while you get changed and in bed."

She was glad it was dark so he couldn't see her fiery blush.

She had to move the green dress to the front part of the wagon so they wouldn't walk into it. She unbuttoned everything and got under the quilt before removing any of it. Then she hurried and pulled her nightgown on. She made sure the covers were pulled up to her chin and she was as far over on the tick as she could get. It was like waiting forever before Declan climbed in.

"*A mhuirnín*, you might want to turn your back while I get ready."

She turned her back to him. "What does *a mhuirnín* mean?"

He hesitated. "It's Gaelic, we speak that in Ireland. It means 'my dear friend.'" He crawled onto the tick and under the covers.

"Good night, *a mhuirnín*."

As he rolled onto his side pointed away from her, she thought for sure she'd stay awake all night, but the heat and stillness of him put her right to sleep.

IT WAS foggy and misting rain in the wee hours of the morning. Declan took one more long admiring gaze at his wife. She sure was pretty with her hair down. He quickly dressed and left the wagon. He picked up two pails and walked toward the Platte River and filled them. The water was moving fast.

It reminded him of many a morning in Mayo, Ireland, and for a second he was homesick, though what he truly yearned for was the Ireland he had known before the rents increased and then the Famine. On top of that it was the worst winter they'd had in years. So many were homeless, the workhouses were overflowing with people waiting in line night and day to get in. There was much sickness too. His mind drifted to how many hundreds of thousands of people had likely died in the workhouses. Things hadn't been just or fair for the people in Ireland. People often wondered why they didn't improve the houses they lived in. But each improvement they made would belong to the landholder. In turn, the landholder, believing he could get a higher rent with such a fine house, often had the people forced from the home they'd just put money into.

People had learned the hard way, and now no one was that foolish. Where was the incentive to live better? The more a man made, the more that was taken from him. Declan had never seen mercy at all, and it had been a good choice to come to America, but he missed his fellow Irishmen; men who knew how he felt, because their lives had been filled with tragedy too.

He started walking back with the filled buckets. Heath was already up and checking on the animals. Zander was nowhere to be seen. He was probably sleeping the whiskey off somewhere. Declan smiled as he drew closer to the wagon. Luella was already at work building up the fire, and it looked as though she had the coffee ready to boil. She was an asset.

"How are you feeling this morning?" he asked. He set the pails down and kissed her cheek.

"I'm getting stronger every day." A smile lit her face. "Good thing, since I have a lot to do today."

She got out the ingredients to make fried cornmeal mush. It was quick and easy until she learned where everything was. She'd seen the men eat and knew she needed to cook plenty. She got busy and smiled at both Heath and Zander when they joined them. They helped themselves to the coffee and then Declan and Heath talked about the horses.

Zander watched her, though, and it made her nervous, the way his eyes followed her. At one point the grease splattered and burned her hand. He never said a word, just watched. The burn was hardly anything, but Declan hurried over and pressed a wet cloth on it.

"Does it hurt?"

"I'm fine it goes with cooking, getting burned a time or two I mean."

She started to pile the pieces of mush on a plate and put more batter in the grease. When she turned around, Zander had helped himself to most of what she had cooked. She hid a sigh of frustration. It wouldn't do to get mad.

"*A mhuirnín*, save some for the rest," she said with a laugh, as she recalled the words Declan had said meant *my dear friend*. "They're hungry too."

Zander stared at her saying nothing. After a moment, she turned away and went back to her task.

Finally, he stood. "Do you call all men that?" he hissed. "I bet in your native tongue you do. I'm beginning to see a side of you I don't think worthy of Declan."

She was going to be sick. She ran away from the wagons and bent over. There wasn't much in her stomach but what little was there came up. Thankfully, she still had the wet cloth Declan had handed her, and she wiped her mouth. Luella couldn't bring herself to go back. She saw Cora wave to her from the other wagon and decided to go that way.

Cora made her sit and handed her a cup of water.

"What happened? Don't you feel well?" Cora's brow furrowed.

"No, nothing to worry about. I'm sure I'll be just fine."

"What happened?" Cora shook her head and laid a gentle hand on Luella's shoulder. "I know you."

"Zander implied I was a sweet talking type of woman, if you know what I mean. My father never allowed me to go anywhere without him. I never—and Zander… Last night he pulled me into an embrace and I was afraid he wouldn't let me go. This morning he took almost all the fried mush I'd made, and when I reminded him there were others eating, I called him a dear friend in Gaelic, and he took offense to it." Unable to catch her breath, she gulped air. "I'm sorry. Everything has happened too fast lately, and my mind is whirling. He wanted to know if I use that sweet talk on all men. It made me sick."

"Declan is coming over. I'm going to go in the wagon and check on Essie." Cora patted her on the shoulder and climbed into the wagon.

Luella closed her eyes. She didn't want to see the look on Declan's face. Maybe once married, an Irish woman wasn't allowed to speak to another man or something. If there were rules, she should have been told.

Declan kneeled before her and took her hands in his. "Luella, are you sick? You can come and lie down in our wagon. I could make you some tea or I could go get Mrs. Chapman."

She shook her head and couldn't meet his gaze. She hurt and she wasn't sure what she had done. "When you marry in Ireland, is the wife not allowed to talk to other men?"

"No. Where did you hear that?"

"I don't know what I've done wrong. Zander doesn't like me. He stared at me all morning and he made me nervous."

"You burned your hand."

"I can't blame him for my clumsiness. I had made two batches of fried mush and piled it on a plate as I usually do. I put more in to cook and when I turned he had taken most of the food and put it on his plate. I didn't want to fight or chastise him or anything all I said was *'a mhuirnín*, save some for the rest. They're hungry too,' and he wanted to know if I sweet talk all men. I guess he thinks I'm a loose woman. I must have broken some rule that makes him think I would, would—" She put her hands over her face and wept.

Declan put his arms around her and stroked her back. "It's my fault."

Lowering her hands, she blinked and looked into his eyes. "Wh-what do you mean?"

"*A mhuirnín* means 'my darling,'" he told her with a tender note in his voice. "I said it because I meant it, but then I wasn't sure you'd want me to call you that. That's why I told you it meant 'dear friend.'" He released a gusty sigh. "Look, he had too much to drink last night, and he's miserable to be around."

Emotions surged, and tears flooded her eyes. "So he is miserable when he drinks and miserable the next day too, and it's fine? I'm sorry I'm not usually a watering pot. I guess since he's your friend I wanted him to like me too." She sighed and blinked back the tears. "We should go back so Cora can come out of her wagon."

He stood and helped her up. As they walked back, he put his arm around her waist. Her heart thumped with her fear of what Zander might do next. But their wagon looked deserted, and she relaxed. "Well, I can wash the dishes in peace. I'm also going to wash clothes today so give me your dirty clothes."

"It'll be nice to have clean clothes. Thank you." He reached into the wagon. "I bought this for you yesterday."

"Declan Leary, how much did you think to spend on me?"

He shrugged his left shoulder. "This is more practical."

She removed the brown paper wrapping, delighted by a sewing needle and some spools of thread, and several lengths of fabric. "I'm good with a needle. I can make you shirts and me some dresses."

A smile broke over his face. "So you approve?"

"Oh, very much so. We can wear these clothes for a very long time. Thank you, Declan."

"Your smile is very becoming."

Her face heated. She fussed with the brown wrapping so she wouldn't have to look up. "Don't forget your dirty clothes."

DECLAN HAD SPENT most of the early part of the day checking the feet of the livestock. He checked the shoes and in some cases put new ones on. Even the oxen were shod. His next plan was to make sure the wagons were in good shape. The metal around the outside of each wheel had to be maintained, and the axles needed to be greased and inspected for any cracks. The canvas needed to be free of threadbare spots. It wouldn't do to have a wagon break down when they were on the trail. When he finished that wagon, he'd make sure the wagon Harrison drove was in good condition too.

When he looked around, he chuckled. Damp, clean clothes hung everywhere. He should have strung a line for Luella. Most women were finished with their laundry, but she still had a pile next to her to finish. Smiling he headed for her. She looked upset. She was used to hard work, so he didn't think it was that. Had someone said something to her?

"I will string a couple lines for you."

She stood up. "That will help, thank you. I'd like to hang these before I do more."

"Those aren't my clothes. Did something happen?"

She shook her head. "No, Zander and Heath were late dropping off their clothes. I thought I was done, but I wasn't."

"I bet your arm hurts."

She didn't say anything as she got back on her knees and continued to scrub a pair of trousers that looked like they hadn't been washed in months. She tried to school her expression, but he saw the pain in her eyes.

He took the trousers out of her hands and let them fall to the ground. He helped her to stand then swung her up into his arms and set her on the tailgate. "Did you tell them to bring their clothes for you to wash?"

"It hadn't occurred to me, but I'm happy to do it, only... I'm not as healed as I thought." She stared at the ground, not meeting his gaze, as though she'd done something wrong.

"Look at me," he ordered softly. "You're my wife, not theirs. They washed—or it looks like didn't wash—their own clothes. Heath and I always did our own. I never paid much attention to what Zander did. He presumed a lot by bringing his clothes here. Heath too, for that matter. You sit and rest. I'll get you some water, get the line strung and the clothes hung."

She didn't say a word, and he was happy she didn't object to his plan. He offered her a cup of water, and she sipped it then handed it back and he took his own sip.

Why did Zander treat Luella like a servant? If he had asked, it would have been different. Luella probably would have tried anyway. She was a sweet generous woman, and she didn't need anyone taking advantage of her good nature. But presuming without even asking... It made Declan's temper flare. Both Zander and Heath knew she'd been hurt. She hadn't quite finished their bedding and a couple of his shirts, so he set about washing the last of their laundry.

He tried not to show his anger, though. As he scrubbed and rinsed, he talked to her about the weather and how it had reminded him of Ireland that morning. Finally, he was done with the wash. He poured the water out of the wash tub and left the clothes on the ground. Heath and Zander could wash their own things.

Finished with the laundry, he went about his maintenance of the wagon, explaining it to her as he went along. He greased the axle and checked each wheel, went over the canvas and repaired a few places where it had worn thin over the ribs.

Once the wagon maintenance was out of the way and the

other wagon seen to, he set up the tent for them for sleeping in that night.

He wasn't quite through with securing the stakes, when Captain London rode up. "Got some buffalo meat from the hunt this morning." He held out a portion without dismounting.

Luella stepped forward and accepted the meat with a shy smile. "Thank you."

"Your first day married," Captain London said. "How's it working out?"

"So far we're doing well," Luella said, widening her smile.

"Good, good. I have plenty more wagons to get to." He nodded to her then to Declan and went over to the next wagon.

"It looks like enough for buffalo steaks," she said.

"I'm making dinner. I'll go see how many will be here before I start cooking." He kissed her and then walked off. He had a couple of men to see and hold conversations with about their treatment of his wife.

He ran into Heath first, resting under a tree with his back against the trunk, twirling a long blade of prairie grass between his thumb and forefinger. Dropping the grass, he sat up and met Declan's stormy gaze with a frown. "Bee crawl in your hat?"

"No," answered Declan easily. "I finished looking over the oxen and the wagons. You handling your responsibilities?"

Heath nodded, shooting Declan a wary glance.

"Luella has certainly been busy," continued Declan, struggling to hide his irritation. "Though I'm a bit concerned. It wasn't long ago that she was injured, and she doesn't yet have all of her strength back."

A scowl darkened Heath's face. "I hadn't realized. I haven't seen her since breakfast, but I'll lend a hand where needed."

Declan contemplated his brother. "You didn't bring your clothes for Luella to wash?"

Heath's jaw dropped and his eyes widened. "Why would I do that? She's not my wife. Besides, it's your first day married. Why? Did something happen?"

"Zander dropped his and your clothes off for Luella to wash," Declan ground out through clenched teeth. "The pain I saw on her face had me hurting for her. A few of the women take in wash for money, but he offered nothing, just expected her to do the extra work." He shook his head. "I just don't know why he dislikes my wife so much."

"He said something about her thinking she can sweet talk her way through life."

Declan nodded. "That was my fault. I called her *a mhuirnín.* Then I realized it was too soon to say such things. I told her it mean dear friend. She called Zander *a mhuirnín* this morning when she was serving breakfast."

Heath threw his head back and laughed. "I guess Zander doesn't want to be her darling." It took a few minutes before he stopped laughing. "Did Zander have a liking for her before you married her? Truthfully, I never took much notice of her except for the scolding she got from her father." He shrugged. "She seems nice enough, and I'm glad you like her."

"Yes… I… like her." Declan nodded and then directed the conversation to a somewhat safer topic. "Captain London dropped off some meat from this morning's hunt. I'm cooking supper tonight and we will eat only our share."

"Wait." Heath stood, a frown wrinkling his brow. "How much did Zander eat this morning? As far as I could see, there wasn't much cooked."

"It sounded to me he ate half of what she made. I'm not sure she even ate. I told her to rest." He turned to walk away but paused and glanced over his shoulder. "You might want to get someone to wash your clothes for you."

Heath nodded rapidly. "No problem. I'm sorry your day isn't going as well. But the horses have all been fed and brushed down. A couple of the mares are carrying. We should be in Oregon before the foals are born. I don't know which stallion it was. They're all of good breeding, so I doubt Harrison will care. There's no way to keep the animals separated out here."

Declan nodded. "We're just fortunate none saw fit to fight over the mares. I'll see you for supper. There're biscuits and bacon for the noon meal." With a final nod at his brother, he went in search of Zander.

He found him at the river skipping stones across the surface. He looked to be in a snit.

"Been looking for you, Zander," Declan barked. "You'll need to find someone to do your laundry. My wife tired herself out on your filthy pants."

Zander opened his mouth, but Declan waved him into silence.

"I asked, and she made no offer to do your laundry. She's not doing any extra work. She's regaining her strength. It's disrespectful to treat my wife like your servant, and it'll happen no more."

Zander's mouth quirked up on one side. "In case you didn't know it, she's been showing interest in me. You should have heard what she called me this morning." He smirked. "You'll need to put a leash on her."

"I already know what was said, and I had told her it meant 'dear friend.' She was trying to be nice to you even though you ate most of the food she had prepared." Declan stepped closer. "You made a scene last night grabbing her from me and trying to dance with her. You hurt her. What have you got against her?"

"Fine. She hardly acknowledges me." Zander spat into the river. "She thinks she's better than me. I tried to give her a ride a few times so she wouldn't have to walk, but she only shook her head and kept walking. Then she ignored me. She's just like her father, thinking the rules don't apply to him. I've known people like her all my life. The Indian would have taken her down a peg and put her in her place."

"You're wrong," Declan ground out, glaring at his old friend. "Luella is sweet and generous. She doesn't think she's good enough for anyone. Her father browbeat her at every turn. Didn't you hear the constant yelling at their wagon? Everyone got to rest but her. She wasn't allowed to talk to any male and taking you up on your offer would have ended badly for her. When she was hurt and unable to work, her father wanted nothing to do with her." He drew a deep breath. "So I don't think your claim of her thinking she's better than anyone is true. But I would have thought the fact that she is my wife would have been enough for you to treat her kindly." He shook his head and strode away, unable to continue the conversation.

Zander's explanation was weak. There were plenty who thought themselves better than the Irish. It was the way of things. But he was mistaken about Luella.

"Declan!" called Zander across the distance between them. "You might want to make sure she's not carrying already. Jimmy Tomlin was meeting her at night when the others were asleep. I saw them with my own eyes. Plain and simple, she's playing you for a fool."

Declan's steps faltered. He felt gut kicked. Who else had seen her and Tomlin? Had she been so desperate to get away from her father she offered her favors to a man she thought would marry her? His hands clenched into fists. Zander could be a fool, but he wasn't a liar.

Shaking his head, he walked farther down the river and watched the water rush by. His chest grew tight, and it became hard to breathe. *Zander* wasn't the fool, *he* was the fool. Her father must have known she was carrying and that was why he wanted her away from the rest of them. She had said she jumped from the wagon. But maybe her father had pushed her. Both Tomlin and Luella had blond hair but Tomlin's eyes were brown. Any child wouldn't look like Declan at all and there would be a scandal. Did Tomlin know he would maybe be a father? Declan kicked the ground, sending a shower of tiny pebbles through the air. He hated lies more than almost anything else.

Alana had always been honest. Her face told everyone what she was thinking. Most days she smiled as bright as the sun. Before the blight on the potatoes he'd saved every cent. He wanted to provide for Alana. The ache in his heart renewed. He could picture her smiling at him with her twinkling blue eyes. An arrow of pain shot through him, and he almost doubled over from it all.

Lord, what am I to do now? I know Alana is dead, but she's still in my heart. I thought my heart was filling with feelings for Luella, but I can see that's been a mistake. I don't have a choice but be her husband, but I don't have it in me to give her affection and smiles. I don't want to confront her either. She'll cry and I'll end up feeling sorry for her. There are many months left until we get to Oregon. I tied myself to her for life, but is she still seeing Tomlin? Lord, help me turn my heart into stone so I don't lash out at her. She was sick this morning, and now I know it must be because she is carrying. I don't want to harm her child, for he is an innocent. Please help me through this.

He swallowed hard and waited for his moist eyes to dry before he went back to make the noon meal.

"WHAT ARE YOU DOING?"

She turned from the tailgate and smiled. "I thought cornbread would go nicely with the steaks."

He frowned. "Please go in the wagon and rest for a bit."

Something was wrong, she could feel it. "It's too hot in the wagon. I'll go and sit by the river for a spell."

He nodded. "Stay where I can see you."

The terseness in his voice didn't sit well. Had she done something? Studying his face didn't help. His expression of displeasure didn't change. She slowly walked to the river; the mighty Platte River. They'd be crossing it tomorrow. It ran quick and it looked deep.

She sat on a large rock and rested. Was he mad about making supper? She hadn't asked him to, she would have been happy to cook. Was he upset that the noon meal hadn't been set out? Had Zander given him a hard time? It felt as though his mood was directed toward her, but she didn't know him well enough to know for certain.

Three unwed girls sat down not too far from her. Luella had envied their friendship. Mandy Echols, Leona Felton, and Patty Mince. They each had large families and bemoaned all the work that it entailed. They wanted to find husbands, and she often heard them talking about the men in the group. Too bad she never had the time to make friends. They enjoyed each other.

They didn't acknowledge her, not even with a nod, and that was unusual. They were nice enough to everyone, so why did it feel as if they were ignoring her? Luella went on staring at the river, but their voices drifted to her.

"It's not true. Can you imagine? He would be at the bottom of my list," Patty said.

"He likes to peek into wagons when women are changing." Mandy said. "Captain London caught him."

"We don't know the whole story. Maybe her father sold

her to Tomlin like he did to that Indian." Leona commented. "It's a real shame she took the best looking man for herself."

"He *is* very nice looking. He learned a lesson about being too nice the hard way. I can't imagine any happiness coming from their union. He got into a fight with Zander." Mandy sighed.

"It's too bad he didn't know the truth before he married her. My mother will be looking for me. I'd best help." Patty stood. "We might as well all go," she suggested.

Luella sat very still. The truth about what? Why did they think her father had sold her to Tomlin, of all people? None of it made sense. Was that why Declan had been cold to her? No, he wouldn't believe a story like that. It would be best forgotten.

She'd sat for some time, though she had gotten little rest. Would it be enough to satisfy Declan? It was almost supper time anyway, so she stood and watched the people around the wagons. Most were work weary, but at least they'd had a day to rest. She put a smile on her face; she was the "happy bride," after all. It would be awkward eating with Zander, but she'd get through it. And then she wanted to heat enough water so she could take a bath in the washtub, but she wouldn't bother Declan about it now.

It was funny how happiness could be so close as to be almost within reach, and then a body was suddenly alone and trying to figure out what to do next. Out of the corner of her eye, she spotted movement, turned and saw Tomlin approaching her. She hastened her steps hoping to avoid him, but he was faster and caught up, grabbing her arm in a punishing grip and yanking her backward.

"I don't know what you're playing at," he snarled, "but people seem to think I took advantage of you." He shook her. "You know that's not true. I want the gossip stopped. I don't know who got you pregnant, but it sure wasn't me." He pushed her aside as he let go and left.

Tremors rocked her body. It was obvious he'd meant business, but she didn't know what he was talking about. Pregnant? Was *that* what people were saying? What those girls had meant?

A few weeks ago she had been invisible to everyone. Now she was the main attraction and it was uncomfortable. Everyone stared at her as she approached the wagon, and she stopped. She looked each person in the eye. She'd done nothing wrong, and she would not act shamed.

Finally, she spotted her husband and some of her panic waned. Watching him, she waited for him to come and escort her back to the wagon, but he stared at her too. She wasn't worldly enough to know what was going on or what to do. The only thing she could do was go to the wagon.

She wanted to hold her head up high but found she couldn't. She stared at her feet as she walked to the wagon. Once there she climbed into the back and lay on the tick with a handkerchief pressed against her mouth. She was half afraid she'd sob so loud the whole camp would hear her.

As far as she could figure, her only crime was jumping out of the moving wagon and getting hurt. It had been a jumble since then, landing her where everyone thought she wasn't moral. She had been raised with the word of God, and she'd never be with anyone but her husband.

All of her good behavior and trying not to chafe at her father's overprotectiveness had turned out to be for naught. Though it had brought her closer to God's love. He'd been the only one she could bare her heart to. He knew what was in her heart now.

Please Lord, help me understand what is going on and how people can believe I've been a loose woman. When would I have had time? From before first light until long after dark I did my chores. I was never left alone. My father won't speak up for me. What about Declan? Oh Lord, please don't let him think those awful things about me. Please bring my heart and soul some peace.

A bit of comfort came over her, but her thoughts kept going in a big circle. She heard Heath and Declan speaking in low tones. It grew darker and darker. After a long while, she took a shuddering breath and put on her nightgown. It was time to get some sleep. They'd be busy tomorrow packing up and traveling to the North Platte Crossing. That was a ferry run and built by Mormons. The river was so fast moving, but God would keep them safe. It would take them a week to ten days of traveling along the south side of the Platte River before they came to the crossing.

CHAPTER FIVE

*D*eclan hadn't had much to say to her in almost a week, and her spirits plummeted. A smile would have been too much to ask. Heath and Zander had made themselves scarce. It was lonely, and Declan volunteered for every guard shift he could. The one night when she thought he'd be there he had offered to bed down with the livestock.

Though he often drove the wagon, she pulled her weight driving it too. It was two hours into the morning on the fifth day out of Fort Laramie, and she was driving the oxen. She was third in line when the first two wagons slowed to a crawl. Upon glancing at a big tree she saw two men swinging from a rope. It didn't seem that they had been there long. She instantly pulled out of the line and jumped down from the wagon. She was promptly sick. Dizziness came upon her. She leaned against the wheel for a moment and then got herself a cup of water.

"If it were Indians, they wouldn't have their scalps. These men must have done something and my guess it has to do with the three graves up ahead," Captain London explained from on top of his big bay gelding.

She nodded and climbed back onto the wagon. Just when she was about to release the brake she heard Declan yell for her to hold up. Nervously, she waited while he tied his horse to the back of the wagon. She moved over as he climbed up.

"Do you want to lie down or is the fresh air better for your morning sickness?"

Her jaw dropped as she recoiled. It was like a slap in the face, and she was at a loss as to what to say. Finally, she sputtered, "I-I wouldn't know! I've only been sick to my stomach twice the whole journey. It was the sight of those men swinging from the tree. The captain said there are three fresh graves up ahead, and he figures it's all ties together. I can drive."

"Maybe after the nooning. I want to be sure you stay healthy."

She turned her head and watched the fir trees as her eyes watered. One tear slipped over and rolled down her cheek. "You never once asked me if the rumors were true. It sounds to me you think I'm carrying a baby. How do you know if I am or if I'm not? You've hardly talked to me for a week. I think I *will* lie down." She turned and climbed over the bench seat into the back of the wagon.

He didn't say a word. Part of her knew he wouldn't but the other part ached for him to say he believed her to be a righteous woman. She was too young to be married. She didn't know how to act or what to do. Sure, she could handle any of the chores. Hard work had been her constant companion. A frustrated sigh escaped. There were so many things she suspected women learned from their mothers she hadn't learned from hers. How did one learn how to talk to a husband?

Cora might be a good choice to talk to, but she hadn't been around as much as usual. Essie had been sick, and they were staying to themselves. It had been hard this past week. How she wished she could have asked her mother's advice.

She reached for Declan's Bible and looked for a passage in Psalms that she recalled. *Psalm 34:17-18. The righteous cry, and the Lord heareth, and delivereth them out of all their troubles. The Lord is nigh unto them that are of a broken heart; and saveth such as be of a contrite spirit.*

God is with me and eventually things will turn out for the best. God brings me comfort. She continued to read. When her eyelids drooped and she could no longer concentrate, she put the Bible back then lay on the tick. The jostling wagon had a way of lulling her, and she let her eyes close.

WHEN SHE WOKE, the wagon was still. Oh no! How long had she slept? A smoky smell from the cook fires drifted in, and she groaned. Scrambling, she put the tailgate down and exited. The fire had been built, its flames burning bright as smoke trailed upward, but there was no sign of her husband. A squeezing sensation pinched at her heart. Swallowing hard, she went about the preparations for supper. She set up the tripod over the fire and hung a large pot full of water. Peeling potatoes only took a short time. She cut them into smaller pieces and added them to the boiling water in the pot. There was elk meat left from the night before that she added along with jarred green beans. She added a dried basil leaf and a chopped wild onion to it.

She'd been proud of her onion find but had no one to share her excitement with. The bread dough she'd made that morning was ready to cook in the Dutch oven and when she peeked in the butter churn she smiled. Who knew that making butter could be so easy? Declan liked butter on his bread and was always bringing milk to her in the mornings. She wouldn't need to make any tomorrow.

There was bound to be extra bread, and bread pudding sounded good for the next evening. Last, she put the coffee on to boil. It all smell delicious but there was no one to share it with. She pulled out the pieces to the tent and set it up. Maybe if she was away from the wagon Declan would feel more comfortable about eating there.

After she put everything she needed in the tent, she filled a plate and brought that inside as well. Essie's pitiful cries nearby tugged at her heart. Luella ate a bit and then went to see what was going on.

Cora's eyes were bloodshot with dark circles under them, and Harrison looked edgy and sad all at the same time.

"What's going on?"

"They just buried Mrs. Chapman and her husband. She hadn't been able to tend Essie in days and the poor little one is so weak." Cora burst out in tears.

"Is it the cough?"

"Mrs. Chapman mentioned whooping cough. I've never heard of it."

"Cora, do you have honey?"

"Yes…"

"Good I'll be right back. I know something that will help." Luella ran to her wagon and grabbed the rest of the onions. Without sparing a glance at Declan, Heath, or Zander, she hurried back to Essie.

Harrison handed her the honey, Luella set it on the tail-gate, and then she went to work. She mixed the juice from the onion with some honey. "This needs to sit for four hours and when it's ready give one teaspoon a day. Now I need to heat some water."

Harrison immediately hopped up and took a pan with hot water off the fire grate and brought it over.

"This, you can do often. You mix honey with warm water and then you can give it to Essie when she fusses. It should help with the cough. I found wild onions yesterday so I'll look for more. If anyone has ginger or chamomile, it can be used in place of the onion. Oh, and fresh garlic can do the same. Someone may have a feeding bottle. I'd ask around but no one will talk to me…"

Tears ran down Cora's face. "You've been like a sister to me. Harrison will ask around and ask the captain if he knows. I know you've been going through a hard time." She released a heavy sigh. "I may have to drip it into her mouth from a spoon."

"I'm sorry to hear about the Chapmans," Luella said softly.

"We are too."

"If you need me, I'll be in the tent tonight. Don't ask. Things are complicated. I'll check on you all tomorrow. Get some sleep," Luella told Cora.

Cora bestowed Luella with one of her beautiful smiles. It made Luella feel good inside until she turned to go back to the wagon. Heaviness settled on her shoulders as she made her way back. She poured herself a cup of coffee and went into the tent without acknowledging the men around the cook fire.

WHY HAD she put up the tent? He usually wasn't here the whole night and he slept under the wagon between guard duties. But there it stood, reaching to the sky, the flicker of a candle inside playing on the canvas wall. Had she found out he had tonight off and was waiting in the tent for him? Zander gave him a speech every night about keeping his hands off his wife because she might bear another man's child.

Declan didn't need to ask her; he already knew she was

indeed pregnant. She'd almost fainted today after she was sick. The whole train had probably watched her. He was so tired of the expressions of sympathy mixed with smirks from the people he traveled with. How was he to have known about her condition? It never once came up before they married. In fact, it still hadn't been talked about. He could ask her about it, but he didn't want to face the truth.

With a sigh he pulled back the flap and went into the tent. The candle flame danced with the breeze that followed him inside. He had expected her to be asleep, but instead, she sat up with her gloriously thick hair shrouding her as she read his Bible.

Shame washed over him. He hadn't been very Christian in his actions toward her. She was his wife. He'd married her before the Lord. His mother, bless her, would have his hide if she knew how he'd been behaving.

"I thought you'd be asleep," he said with a raspy quality to his voice.

"Oh!" She glanced up with a look of surprise on her face. "I didn't know you'd be here. I never know what your schedule is." She went back to reading.

He undressed and got into bed next to her. He probably shouldn't interrupt her reading, so instead he lay on his side watching her. She was the picture of innocence. It was very deceiving... and depressing.

Finally, she lay the Bible down and blew out the candle. She put her head on the pillow and lay on her side with her back toward him.

"We can't go on like this," he murmured. "Your home should be a place you want to be, not a place you avoid. It's time for you to tell the truth."

She stiffened and was quiet for a while. "It's very sad about the Chapmans. And Essie is very sick."

"Yes, I know. What I'm referring to is the baby you're carrying. You should have told me."

"There's nothing to tell."

He balled his fists. He couldn't make her tell him. "I think there is plenty you need to say."

"Good night."

He lay on his back staring at the tent ceiling. His frustration knew no bounds, but he stewed in silence. She'd been yelled at by her father enough to last a lifetime. She'd looked like she was afraid of Tomlin too. Maybe her father had sold her for a few nights. He just didn't know. It had been so easy with Alana. She'd known what he was thinking, often before he did, it had seemed.

He turned until he was facing Luella's back. She wasn't a deceitful woman, and if something had happened, he didn't believe it was of her choosing. Sighing, he reached out and pulled her to him. He enclosed her in his arms and held her.

After a moment, her body shook, and he knew she was sobbing. He didn't let go. They had a lot to figure out but they would have to get everything out in the open so the healing could begin. Hopefully, she had found a passage in his Bible to give her some peace.

He needed his sleep since he was driving the stock across the river. He'd volunteered for the dangerous job. Now he wished he hadn't. He hadn't given Luella one thought. It was his responsibility to see that she made it across safely. He'd been a fool to allow his anger to get in the way of decision making.

It had been a scenic ride to the Mormon ferry, yet hard. They were forever going up only to go back down and then up again. The animals were tired. The mountains in their view were a spectacular sight and he'd even seen roses growing.

They'd all been warned of the high price they'd have to

pay to cross the Platte using the ferry but there wasn't any choice. It was almost certain death to try to ford the river. Five dollars was a very dear price to pay but not as much cost as a single life.

They woke the next morning and hurried to pack. The captain wanted an early start crossing. They could rest on the other side, he kept explaining.

Declan didn't like the look of the water. It seemed to be moving more rapidly than it had been the day before. He was probably making something out of nothing, he admonished himself. People crossed the river all the time. He stopped by the wagon before he rounded up the livestock.

Luella was busy, moving efficiently and with a purpose, but there was a sadness to her that made his heart hurt. She stood as though rooted in one spot as he walked to her. Then he pulled her into his arms and held on.

"You take care crossing," he said gruffly.

She gave a start of surprise. "You're not driving the wagon?"

"I drew the short straw, and I'll be driving the livestock across. Heath will go across the ferry with you. Be careful."

She pulled back and stared up into his eyes. "You have a care too." She hugged him close and hard for a moment and then let go.

He stepped back and gave her a nod. "I heard what you did for Essie. You're a good woman." Then he walked away wishing he was taking her over on the ferry.

Before he could think too much more, he mounted his horse and drove the livestock toward the bank of the river. He and two other drovers urged the animals into the surprisingly cold water and it took all their strength to keep on their mounts and drive the livestock across. The natural inclination was to go downstream with the force of the water, but they finally got all of them over with no mishaps.

They drove the animals another mile or so out to a location the captain described as the stopping point. Declan wished he could get off his horse and plop down to rest but he needed to check on his wife.

He rode up to the bank and began to talk to Earl, one of the men who ran the ferry.

"You did right well getting those beasts across. We usually lose at least one man each crossing. Yesterday was bad. We lost two wagons. One had only had a man on it and he swam for it and survived. The other had a family of four and they are with God now." He took a breath and stared across the river. "I'm praying for your group."

Declan stepped away from the man. He'd known there would be some risk, but no one told him just how treacherous it would be. His mind was occupied with only one thought. Who was driving Luella?

He watched as the first half of the group crossed. There were too many near misses, and his nerves became stretched to their limits. Luella drove the next wagon. Wait! What had happened? Why was she driving the wagon? Fear and anger filled him. The ferry tipped as she drove the wagon onto it. Then it righted. He held his breath, and then she saw him and smiled.

The next thing he knew the wagon was on its side in the harsh water. He couldn't catch a glimpse of Luella anywhere. He leaped on his horse and rode along the river bank. He thought he saw her blue dress, but it disappeared so quickly he might have imagined it. The wagon smashed to pieces as it hit three large boulders. Panic filled him, his heart beat a staccato rhythm, blood pounding in his ears as he searched the churning water.

He spurred his mount on, frantically searching the water, the rocks, the banks, his breath coming in frenzied bursts. He had to locate her. He rode for at least another hour before

Heath caught up to him.

"Did you find her?" Declan asked.

"No, there's been no sign of her. All the things that were in the wagon are gone too."

"Why weren't you the one driving the oxen? Why was Luella holding the lines? Where were you?" His voice almost broke.

"Rod Waverly had taken ill and Luella insisted I drive their wagon instead of his wife Sally. Zander got bogged down putting a new wheel on Leo Span's family wagon. He said he didn't know he was supposed to check the wheels and repair them. Let's ride. I didn't see any sight of her coming here to you."

Declan nodded to Heath, but he couldn't speak.

"We'll find her Declan."

They rode for hours, often doubling back in case they'd missed her somehow. Less and fewer debris from the shattered wagon floated by. Most of it had already sunk. Maybe she'd somehow made it to the bank. Maybe she's gotten out of the water. It was a warm day, but the water had been freezing cold.

He heard the pounding of horses running toward him and looked up, grateful to see more men from the wagon train coming to help.

Please Lord.

Harrison and Zander were among them.

"Anything?" Harrison asked. He looked as worn as Declan felt.

"No, I thought I saw something the color of her dress but it was gone in a flash. You should be with Cora and Essie."

"Thanks to your wife, Essie is breathing better than she has in days. Most of the wagons have gone on to camp at the spot you were at. The captain has made a huge fire hoping if she's lost she'll see it." Harrison sighed, seeming to not know what to say. "I'm so sorry, Declan, I wish I had more to say."

Declan swallowed hard, trying to be brave. "Do you think it's possible she got this far? The river is swift, but there are also many boulders to get by."

"The ferry operators only spared one man to ride the bank on their side. It was more important that they get everyone across the river—to them at least. We didn't even know anything happened until we reached this side. I asked her father about it and he's not one to be cheerful."

"How do you want to proceed?" Zander asked Declan.

"Heath, go back and get supplies for the both of us. I'll stay along the river and stop when it gets dark. You can catch up with me. A few of you can sweep the area around the bank for any sign of someone getting out of the water. Harrison, if you and Zander could take the ferry back to the other side and check the bank there..." He stared at the churning water. "Heath and I will spend a couple days looking. Then we'll catch up with you."

Heath took off before Declan was finished. "I appreciate you all coming out here. If a few could stay by the fire this evening before you move on tomorrow I'd appreciate it." He didn't know what else to say.

Harrison took over. "We all have our duties mapped out for us; we might as well go about them. I hope we find her Declan."

"Me too." He turned his horse around and slowly proceeded down the river. "Me too," he whispered.

The mosquitos were getting thick, and they made an already intolerable situation even worse. He found a stick and hit bushes next to the river with it. He only ended up scaring a few animals. Where was she? He continued on into late afternoon, though he began to doubt she'd gotten this far.

Then he saw it; a round gold ring on the ground. He immediately jumped down and snatched up the ring then studied the area before he walked over any tracks. He could see two sets of prints. One of them wore moccasins. From what he could tell, the man had helped her out of the water. They had taken a few steps and then he'd picked her up and carried her.

Declan followed the footprints until they stopped at a set of unshod hoof prints from probably an Indian pony. The Indian had made no attempt to hide the tracks so Declan knew which direction they were traveling in. North.

He needed to leave a trail for Heath. He saw gray yarn snarled up in a bush and tried his best to untangle it. Next he hung long pieces from branches He tied the ring to one of them. After that, every half mile or so he hung another. He was aware that he was steadily climbing through sand. He could see a long way, yet there was no sign of Luella. He turned to go back toward the river so his horse could graze and get some much needed rest. What seemed to be a small game path off the main trail caught his eye, and he saw the dress she'd worn all torn and mangled and thrown on the ground.

He jumped off his horse and drew his gun. He turned in a slow circle but saw no one. Breaking down and weeping was not an option, maybe she was still alive. If she was, she would need him to have his wits about him. He picked up the dress and studied the ground. There appeared to have been a scuffle, but he saw no sign of her being pushed to the ground. That was a good thing. He stood there listening, striving to hear something, anything that would give him hope. But the only sound was the rushing of the confounded river. He walked in a circle and tried to find their tracks. He found a few of the beads like the ones used to decorate their clothes strewn on the ground, and he headed in that direction.

Heath would never be able to find him now. If anything happened to Heath too…

Had Eagle Nest taken her? Was she still alive? He could kick himself for listening to others' falsehoods against her. She never once gave him reason to doubt her. He should be horse whipped for his actions. He should have stayed by her side and stared down anyone who dared to say anything unkind. His actions had probably condemned her in their eyes.

He was the one who was no good. Even if she was with child, that child would become his. He'd never turn his back on a wee babe. Her blessing would be his. If only she'd just told him.

He kept to the trail but lost where they had stepped off it. Where could he have taken her? Beyond the trees there wasn't anything to see. They must be in the forest he was in. He went back to where he'd last seen their tracks and began to circle out from that point. If they'd changed direction, he hoped to find some indication of it so he could follow.

His eyes moistened as he imagined all the things that could be happening to her, his wife, his *a mhuirnín*, his *grá mo chroí*.

Please Lord, keep her safe.

The sun would begin its descent all too soon. She could be dead and he'd never know, just like Alana. He took a deep breath. Alana good bye to ye lass. You filled my heart for more than half my life. *Slán as anois, Good bye for now. If anyone is with the good Lord, it's you.*

"Declan! Declan you fool where are you?"

He turned to the sound of his brother's voice and rode toward it.

Heath jumped down from his mount with Luella's wedding band in his hand. "You need to come with me and give this back to your wife!"

Declan slide down to the ground. "What?"

Heath caught him in a big bear hug. "She's alive, so very alive and wants you."

Declan felt the smile spread across his face. He took the ring from Heath and put it on his little finger. "What are we waiting for?"

They both mounted, and he wished he could run the horse the whole way but that was no way to treat a horse that had helped him all day. Finally he could see the fire by the bank. He wanted to know what happened, but Heath said it wasn't his story to tell except that she was unharmed.

He didn't wait for the bay to come to a full stop before he had both feet on the ground. There she was, her hair wet, and she was wrapped in a blanket. He'd never seen a grander sight. His heart beat quickened as he closed the distance between them. He put his hands on her cheeks and stared into her shimmering blue eyes.

He felt his own tears on his cheeks as he leaned forward and placed his lips upon hers. So many emotions filled him as he pulled her closer. Love, relief, and thankfulness. He was oh, so grateful. He'd thought deep down he'd never see her again.

"*Grá mo chroí*," he whispered in her ear before he let her out of his embrace. He took her hand. He couldn't take his eyes off of her.

"I'm so glad to see you, Declan. There were a few times I thought my time had come." A shaky smile lit her face. "You are the most handsome man I've ever seen."

Smiling, he scrubbed a hand down his face, not quite managing to suppress a chuckle. She's almost drowned and here she was calling him handsome.

Her smile faded. "My parents? Where are they? Did they help look for me?"

"They went on with the rest of the train to the next camp-site a way ahead."

A great pain crossed her face.

How he wished he hadn't had to tell her that. He took her hands in his and squeezed. "They don't matter. Only you and I matter. Have you eaten? Are you warm enough? What can I get for you? All our things are in the water now, but we'll find a way. I promise we'll get where we're headed."

Cora stood with Essie in her arms. "Harrison and Zander went back to the Mormon post, and you now have a new wagon with what you need. I hope. You know how men can be." She laughed and cried.

Luella reached for Essie and snuggled her close. "You will be just fine, aren't you little one?" She handed the baby to Declan and smiled when he held her.

Harrison walked down to the fire and hugged Luella. Then he took his baby back. "You're parked next to our wagon. You are such a fine sight, Luella and it's nice to see a smile on your face Declan. Bless you both."

"Let's get you into some warm clothes, Luella." Declan swung her up into his arms and headed toward camp. She touched his face and shoulders the whole time as though she was making sure he was real. "I'm told they set a tent up."

"Are you hungry?" he asked.

"I'm more tired than anything, and I want to lay down with your arms around me."

Smiling, he opened the flap to the new tent allowing her to go first. She gasped and he followed her inside. A new tick mattress sat to the side, piled with quilts that the other women must have donated. The one on top was a wedding pattern, one he recognized that his ma had made when times had been a bit easier. A nightgown lay on the bed, and a trunk also had been placed in the tent with a new dress on top of it.

"Oh my. If all I had was you, Declan, it would be more than enough."

He took the blanket from her and was surprised to see her in an Indian dress. Her expression was one of fear. He took a step and held her. "I thought you were taken by Indians. I found your dress."

"Swift Eagle found me — that's his real name, not Eagle Nest. He pulled me half dead from the dark water. I couldn't find which way was up and I couldn't come up for air. He grabbed me and pulled me out. He put my wedding ring on the bank where he pulled me out for someone to find and know I had made it out of the water. There were other Indians about, but he said they weren't as friendly. I must have fainted. I woke and I was wearing this. I got upset, but he explained it was supposed to have been my dress for my wedding to him. He promised he didn't touch me in that way." She swallowed hard. "I—I believe him."

She took her night gown and asked for his help in getting the other dress off. It surprised him she wasn't wearing anything under it. He quickly averted his eyes and put the dress on the trunk as she got her night gown on.

"I believe him," she repeated.

"I do too," he whispered. "He would have taken you with him if he had done anything."

Luella nodded. "I'm grateful to him."

"Are you sure you're fine? What about the baby?"

Her smile faded and she crawled into the bed and under the covers. "There is no baby."

He reeled backwards a step in horror. "It died?"

She turned her back to him. "Unless a miracle has occurred, there is no possible way for me to be with child." She kept her back to him.

"You aren't, I mean weren't...?"

"I was so happy to see you, so happy to be alive. I never

thought you'd make me cry tonight. I've always worked hard and tried to please my parents. I would never—it wouldn't occur to me to— I wasn't brought up that way. Believe it or not, but Cora is the only friend I've ever had." Her words conveyed deep sadness, and he sensed she was close to tears. "It's been such a hard day. I thought my time with you had come to an end and that made me the saddest of all. I don't deserve questions or doubts about my innocence. I only have one way to prove it to you, and right now I don't want to be touched by anyone."

His mouth opened, but he didn't know what to say. She'd told him before that she was pure, and he'd never believed her.

"I hadn't thought about it before, but now people will assume as you did, that I lost the baby. My vindication was to have come when there wasn't a baby—" Her voice broke and she sniffled.

"Did anyone look you over?"

"I said I was fine."

"How could anyone be fine in that river? Tell me you didn't hit a rock or two."

"I did, and more than two." She turned over and looked at him, eyes spilling over, cheeks damp from the tears.

"You have bruises forming on your head," he said.

"I expect so and my shoulders and legs too, and my back feels like the skin has been rubbed off. I didn't hurt much before, but now…"

"Let me check and see what is in the wagon."

He went outside and looked up at the bright moon and the shimmering stars. He'd hurt her and he hadn't meant to. It was concern for her, but she didn't see it that way. He found the medical supplies in the wagon and grabbed salve and bandages and a few cloths. Then he filled a basin with water. He'd have to minister to her.

It would not be easy.

LUELLA TRIED TO STAY STILL, but each time he touched her back she flinched away. She felt Mrs. Chapman's death more keenly than ever now that she was in need. Try as she might, she couldn't get his words out of her head. He'd never believed her about the baby. He had never given her the benefit of the doubt; she just thought he had. If he had told *her* something, she would have believed him. Their marriage was one big mistake that hurt her daily, and the hurt kept growing.

She'd smile and let everyone know how happy they were but she'd always know he didn't trust her. It stung and unlike the abrasions on her body, her heart wouldn't heal as fast if ever. She'd kept herself covered as he tended to her, so he didn't see anything but the one spot he was tending. But one day he might and the thought of that happening embarrassed her. There was no help for it.

She straightened her gown as he put the supplies away and lay down on her side with her back toward him. She hadn't a clue how to be a wife. She didn't want to be a wife anymore, but that wasn't a choice until they reached Oregon. Jumping out of her Pa's wagon had cost her everything. Everyone did it and a few had gotten hurt, but she'd thought she knew what she was doing.

He got into bed and she leaned up and blew out the candle. He moved closer, and she stiffened. He must have noticed because he moved back and put more space between them.

There was so much about what happened she wanted to tell him. Swift Eagle laughed and laughed about being called Eagle Nest. He was a good man, and he'd find himself a good bride. He had told her he was Sioux and he was on his way back to his people. She'd heard such horrible things about them, but he was nothing like those tales. He'd shown her the eagle feathers he'd gotten on his trip and he had given her one. He honored her.

She laughed and cut it short, hoping Declan hadn't heard her unintended noise.

"What's so funny?"

"Swift Eagle thought the name Eagle Nest was very amusing."

"You told him that?"

"Yes. He was a gentleman, and he saved my life. I'm never going to cross a river again."

"I wish we wouldn't have to but there are more to come. I'll keep you safe."

Her eyes welled up again. "Thank you." She wanted to know what *grá mo chroí* meant, but she had her pride.

SHE WOKE the next morning hearing whispers and closed her eyes. Dismay washed over her. Nothing had changed, and her heart ached. Why were some women naturally cheerful and friendly? Others didn't seem to care and kept to themselves. She hadn't noticed any other woman like herself who was longing for a sense of belonging. She did have Cora, and for that she was grateful.

Taking a fortifying breath she sat up, wincing in pain, and then stood. Every muscle screamed and felt weak. She made it to the trunk and sat down. The dress on it was a pretty sky blue calico and she bet the trunk held new under-clothes. She sat for a moment, resting and catching her breath.

Declan entered the tent and his expression turned to one of concern when he saw her. "Hurting?"

"Yes, every part of me." She'd wanted to add including her heart, but she wasn't brave enough to say it.

"Let's get you standing so I can get the rest of the clothes. Cora will be here in a bit to help you." A muscle worked in his jaw as he seemed to struggle with his next words. "Luella, I made a mess of everything last night. I opened my mouth when I should have stayed quiet."

"No, Declan, you should always say what you mean. I just thought we were past the doubts about me, and the hurt went deep. After Cora helps me, I'll get breakfast made."

He got out all she needed and helped her to sit back down. Then he gave her a nod and left her alone.

CHAPTER SIX

"I'd like to walk today. If you'll slow down I can get down," she said to Declan. Those were the first words spoken in at least two hours. They were riding through dry dust, and once in a great while they were lucky to spot a bush.

"I'd rather you sit in the back of the wagon if the dust is too much up here."

"I just need to stretch my legs a bit is all."

He shook his head. "We'll talk about it tonight."

"You mean when we are done for the day? Are you afraid I'll go off with another man?" Her patience was at an end. He'd been treating her like glass for the last two days and refused to allow her out of his sight. At first she thought he was afraid she'd get lost or hurt again, but it finally hit her. He wanted to be sure she wasn't meeting anyone.

The realization battered her spirit. She needed to go talk to the reverend and see about getting a Bible to read. That had brought her such comfort. She had to sleep in the wagon alone and if Declan was on guard duty, Zander or Heath slept under the wagon. But those times when she couldn't sleep, she had appreciated having Declan's Bible for company.

Ahead of them, she spotted Cora walking with Essie; apparently Harrison trusted her.

Luella turned her head and watched the dry earth as they went by. What had she done? God help her but she'd rather be back with her family. At least she knew what to expect day in and day out. Declan never mentioned the future, probably because they didn't have one together. It was hard to pay for unknown sins.

She coughed some dust out of her throat. The air was dry too. They needed to conserve water. There wouldn't be more for a few days. They'd been rationing except for Heath. He thought he needed to wash up. She'd never seen anything like it. Others were also taking baths and washing clothes at night. What happened if a wagon ran out? Was the rest of the party supposed to share their carefully saved water? She would say something to Heath tonight. They'd even had to use their own water for the oxen. Most of the wives and families walked to give the livestock a bit of relief.

She'd seen their eyes widen a bit as she and Declan went by. Yes, she needed a Bible.

A few hours later, as the sun began to rest, they stopped. The captain had warned all of them about the alkali water in the area and how it could make a person sick, but she'd seen people drink it.

The train stopped and she started to climb down.

"Wait." Declan rounded the oxen and lifted her down to the ground. His hands on her waist felt so nice, and that humiliated her. Maybe people just knew by looking at her she was bound to be wanton.

"Will you speak to Heath about using so much water? He's washing up while the rest of us are filthy." she asked. "What if we run out?"

Declan let go of her and nodded. "I will. Don't overdo it. This dust and heat can take a toll on a person."

"Yes." She walked to the back of their wagon and spotted the reverend's wagon. She hurried over to it and spoke to his wife, who was overjoyed to be of help.

Luella smiled walking back to the wagon. Her Bible was brand new and wrapped in a fine piece of cloth.

"Where were you?" Declan looked particularly annoyed.

She furrowed her brow. "Why? I wasn't gone long."

"Just tell me."

She walked around him and put the tailgate down. Then she carefully placed her Bible on the straw tick. Biscuits and bacon didn't take much water, and it was too bad if they've had the same thing for days. They could help themselves to hardtack and dried beef. She'd made the

dough that morning. Now all she needed was to roll it out and cut the biscuits. She readied everything for cooking and then put the coffee on.

Declan hadn't unhitched the oxen. Instead, he watched her. She wiped her brow with her sleeve and went to the front of the wagon. She'd taken care of her family oxen many times. She started unbuckling the leather lines when she felt someone behind her. She turned.

"If you're not going to take care... Oh, Heath what do you want? Are you here to care for the oxen?"

"No. I want you to stay out of my business. I work hard and I'll use as much water as I want. It's not fair to Declan that he got stuck with you. He can't even hold his head up with all the talk about you and the Indian and Tomlin. People claim to have seen you. It's no longer a rumor. It's fact and as soon as the baby is born we'll all know. It's all Zander talks about,"

She shuddered. "I'm not expecting a baby."

"So that's the way of it, eh?" He grunted. "Lost it in the

river? Zander was right then. He thought that might happen. Is that why Eagle Nest gave you back? He wasn't going to be a father after all? Stay out of my business." He stormed away.

Where was Declan? She continued unyoking the oxen. It was heavy work and she was weary, but she got it done. Were they being fed? With what? There wasn't any grass. Other women had gathered buffalo chips to make a fire with. The biggest ox, Victor, moved and knocked her down. It was the last straw. Why couldn't she just sit and cry? Maybe she could crawl under the wagon and weep.

Zander helped her up. "You shouldn't be around the oxen. I'll take care of them. Are you hurt again?"

"I'm fine." She wasn't able to bring herself to look at him. After walking to the back of the wagon, she moved all the food aside and crawled into the back. She held her Bible to her chest and fell asleep.

"I'm telling you to get rid of her. She's making a fool of you! You would never have allowed Alana to carry on the way Luella has."

"I told you to let her be. She's more child than woman, and she was never having a baby."

"Who'd you hear that from?" Heath demanded with a harsh laugh.

"She told me," Declan responded.

"I'm sure she did. She has you wrapped up and believing everything she says."

She'd had enough. The moon was full, so she took a quilt and her Bible and planned to read it away from the wagon. She jumped down, grabbed up some of her things, and marched off. She felt the gazes of the others on her as she kept walking. Her father ran after her and caught her arm, hauling her backward. He shook her and raised his hand. It took most of her strength and she pulled away, crying out in pain, and continued on.

She looked for a spot where there was no wildlife around and spread out her quilt. Next, she sat down and unwrapped her bible. She ran her hand over the front of it and finally she opened it. She read until she felt a bit of peace. She closed the book and turned her face up to the heavens.

Lord I don't think yelling and telling everyone they are wrong will do anything. I try to be a good Christian. I haven't gone around spreading lies. I'm not sure what to do. My heart is being torn apart. Please God, forgive my sins, especially the sin that caused all the lies to be told about me. Thank you for saving me from the river. Please Lord let me know what sin I committed so I don't do it again.

"Praying?"

She turned her head and gazed at Declan. "Yes. I asked Him to show me which sin I committed. It must have been a big one to be treated so badly. I keep thinking and thinking, but I can't think of what I did except for jumping off the wagon. I can't think of any big unkindness I've done. But I must have done something. I suppose whatever I did I didn't know it was bad. No man has touched me so what else can it be? The reverend told me to pray on it, and his wife gave me this Bible today."

He didn't say anything, just stared at her.

"I know you think of me as a child, and I'm sorry I've been such a disappointment to you. You and my father have that in common. I practically raised my younger brothers, and I did most of the chores, but I guess that doesn't mean I'm an adult. I never questioned myself so much before. My father would say something about chores I didn't do correctly. I knew that I did do them the right way, so it didn't hurt much." She lifted her face and met his gaze. "I can't be your wife anymore. I'll sleep under Harrison's wagon or, since they use their tent much of the time, maybe I can sleep in their wagon. I can work for my keep. You'd be free to find a woman of virtue and I, well I could figure out what it is about me that makes me more child than adult. Cora can tell me. I suspect I'll be a different person by the time I get to Oregon. I don't want to be a cause of embarrassment for you. You're a good man, Declan, and you don't deserve to be stuck with me."

A muscle ticked in his jaw, but he said nothing. His quietness made her nervous.

"It's actually very beautiful in this barren land at night. The moon looks bigger. It's been a nice evening in that aspect. Well, should I leave the quilt for you or do you want to walk back with me?" She didn't look at him.

He held out a hand and when she took hold of it, he helped her up. He pulled her in front of him and looked into her eyes. "I knew it had been hard on you, but I did not understand you were hurting this much. I don't want you to change, and I don't want you to leave. We'll work together and make our marriage a good one. I allowed everyone else's lies get into my head, and I'm so very sorry. I had it planned where I'd claim the child as mine and raise it as mine. I'm not stuck with you, *a mhuirnín*. I want to be your husband."

She took her hand out of his and hugged her Bible and quilt to her. "You are a noble man, Declan. I don't know how to fix any of this. I don't have enough experience in life to know if I should go or if I should stay. There is much to admire about you, and I seem to just drag you down." She shook her head. "I don't know how to better myself. I don't know how to be a woman or a wife. I've tried and tried and maybe I haven't tried hard enough but I don't know what else I can do. None of it is your fault. If not for you, well I don't know who I might have ended up with." She blinked twice, hard, against her tears. "I know you have great things in your future with Heath and Zander. You'll all eventually marry and have children who will play with each other.

Zander might have had it right when he gave me all those clothes to wash. People pay to have it done, so maybe I can get a job doing laundry. I can cook, clean and run a farm if necessary. Someone might find that to be an asset. I don't mind hard work, and truthfully, the harder I work the less time I have to dwell on things that can't be. We haven't been talking to each other, and I don't know what will happen between now and when we get to Oregon. I just want you to know I wish you well and I thank you for all you've done to help me. I'll still do my part to get there but after I will not stay with the three of you. My heart has been shredded and I have some healing to do before I could ever trust another or allow anyone to be my friend."

"Luella, please."

"Declan I can't," she interrupted. "I just can't. Besides, I'm waiting on God to reveal the sin I did that led me to such agony. I wouldn't want to repeat it. I don't want Heath or Zander to sleep under the wagon and they can eat after we are done. I can't sit with them and break bread. I'd rather avoid them if I can. I'll sleep in the wagon and you can have the tent. I'll not lay there and listen to you breathe while I long for a life that will never be. I suppose that's the child in me; to yearn and dream. I'll act as though all is fine. I will not shame you. Good night."

She hurried toward the wagons with a huge lump in her throat. The tent had been put up and she took her things out of it and crawled into the wagon. If being an adult hurt so much she'd stay a child for as long as she could. Sorrow filled her as she changed into her night gown and slid under the covers. She picked up her Bible and cradled it into her arms as she prayed for sleep.

DECLAN RAN his fingers through his hair as he sat on the trunk in the tent. What had he done? He'd never seen so much pain before. Even in Ireland the people starving worked and worked but they knew their lot in life. They knew most of them would die. Their anguish was expected and though many tears were spilt, he'd never seen grief as strong as Luella's. It shamed him he never put a stop to the rumors. He just hoped it would all go away. He told her how much he'd loved Alana and the life they had planned, but he had never told Luella he loved *her* or what their future might be. He'd never thanked her for all the work she'd done every day. He admired her but had he once told her? He couldn't remember if he had. She was his wife and he just thought she'd be by his side. He'd thought his heart would break at the river crossing, but it didn't take long before he had once again treated her with mistrust. He swallowed hard. Hearing that she thought she'd brought all of it on herself by some sin she had yet to learn of tore at his soul. Parting from her might be in her best interest. The thought near killed him, but he had to think of her first.

He woke earlier than usual and made the fire. As quietly as he could he got out the coffee pot, coffee mill and beans. The water was down more than he would have thought. He sighed. Either Heath or Zander didn't heed his warning or someone had helped themselves to the water. He took it from the side of the wagon and put it in the tent for now. They'd keep it in the wagon until they found more.

He cooked bacon while the camp came to life. Then he sat on a crate and waited a bit. He stood when he saw Luella and lifted her down from the back of the wagon. He kept his hands on her waist and then he kissed her cheek. She looked into his eyes and he gave her a small smile. He had to go really slow, or he'd lose her forever. Then again, he'd convinced himself to give her up the night before, hadn't he?

"Would you like a cup of coffee?" he asked.

"I must have really overslept. I can get my own, though I do thank you for making it and breakfast—" Her eyes widened in horror. "The water barrel!" She grabbed his forearm.

He put his hand over her hard grip. "I put it in the tent."

She stared at him, dumbfounded.

"I noticed that it was lower than it should be. I'll not hang it on the side of the wagon again until we are able to refill it. You were right, and I should have said something on day one about how we should ration the water. I don't know if it was Heath or Zander, or if it was someone else on the train."

Her eyes gentled and she took her hand off his arm. "I've seen a few drinking the alkali water. I thought we weren't supposed to drink it."

"They'll be sick, and depending on how much they drank, a person could die. I can't wait to be done with this part of the trip. Many animals are sick too."

"Gather round! Gather round!" Captain London yelled from the middle of the wagon circle. Someone brought out a crate and the captain stood on top of it. When a good amount of people gathered he began. "Now I've been encouraging you who have heavy wagons to lighten your loads. Everyone who is able is to walk. The oxen and mules are no good to us if they die. We all know to ration the water. This isn't a vacation, people, this is life and death. Those of you who drank the alkali water will soon be feeling sick, and I know there are some that are already sick." He gestured toward a nearby pair of oxen. "The animals will drink anything so we have to steer them clear of the alkali ponds and streams. Now pack up. We'll stop and rest the animals a bit more today. I can't tell you just how important it is to lighten the wagons. We will be traveling longer into the evening while it's a little cooler if that's possible. Then late the day after next we will reach drinkable water. Don't panic, just be smart. Plenty of people have made it through with no problems. We are all in the same boat and we'll all smell the same by the end of this part of the journey. Water is for drinking only. Now go get packed up and decide what you're going to leave behind. We will be climbing all day."

Declan liked the way Luella looked to him with trust. Her confidence somehow drove him to stand taller and square his shoulders. "We'll be fine," he reassured her.

"I know we will." She beamed at him, but her smile faded as she asked, "Who is sick? I know that a bit of vinegar mixed with flour can be helpful."

"You still want to help people who have caused you nothing but pain?" This way of thinking was foreign to him. His mother had been one to care for others, but too many people crossing his path of late had been the sort who only thought of themselves, their comforts.

"We should always try to help when we can." Her soft words sent a wave of heat into his face.

He took her hand in his and kissed the back of it. "You're a good woman." He let go when they arrived at the wagon.

Heath and Zander were waiting, and both demanded the water. They had heard the same announcement he had, but they didn't seem like they planned to heed the warnings. Shaking his head, Declan took two cups, went into the tent, and dipped water into both of them. He came back out. "This is all we have until afternoon, so I suggest you drink it and not use it to wash. Didn't you listen to the captain just now?"

Zander stared at the ground. "We were too busy trying to decide if you both slept in the wagon since the tick is in there."

Irritation flared. "Let me make this clear," he said in a low voice. "There will be no more speculation about me or Luella. We have a right to our privacy. I don't have time to wonder who slept where. There is always work to do. You both need to see to your responsibilities. What about Harrison's animals? Are you taking care that they stay away from the bad water?"

"Yes, brother, we are. Especially after he bellowed at us yesterday about it." He leaned forward and got in Declan's face. "So, let me get this straight, you let her tell you what to do with the water?"

It was a struggle, but Declan managed to answer in a level but firm manner. "We discussed it together after I saw that someone was taking more than their share last night. If you want water, you need to ask for it."

Heath clenched his teeth. "I think that trunk in there is a bit too heavy." He reached in and pulled it out of the wagon and let it fall onto the ground. All of Luella's things fell into the alkali-covered sand, even her Bible.

She stood horrified but never said a word. She rescued her Bible and climbed to the front bench. She sat reading as though nothing happened.

"What is wrong with you? Heath, you are acting like a bear with a thorn in its paw," Declan hissed.

"How would you like to be the one defending your brother and his questionable wife? All day every day someone has something to say, and I'm not allowed to punch any of them in the face. My temper is hard enough to rein in. I'm tired of it. You could leave her behind instead of the trunk—or with the trunk. No woman will ever tell me how much to eat or how much water I can have. I'm a man, proud and strong. You used to be the proudest of all but look at you now. You dance to her tune, and she's made you foolish and weak. When we get to Oregon, you go one way and I'll go another."

Declan stood still without saying a word. He refused to back down. He and Heath had always had their arguments but nothing like this. And why was it anyone's business what was going on with Luella? He hurt for Luella, for Heath, and for Zander. Looking around, he saw more people watching him.

His Irish temper bubbled to the surface. "Can't you mind your own business? Your suspicions and lies are breaking my family apart, and they are all I have left in this world. Just let it be, will ya?" He righted the trunk and put his wife's scant belongings back in it. An eagle feather fell out of one of her garments and fluttered to the ground, and he smiled. The Indians did not give such gifts lightly; they must be earned. Swift Eagle must have thought her worthy, and he was right. His wife was fine and brave.

Still grasping the eagle feather, Declan strode to the front of the wagon and peered up at his wife. He held out the feather. With a shaky smile, she took the feather in her hand and slid it inside her Bible.

"Luella, will you come down and help me?" he asked gently.

"Of course, I'll be right there." She accepted his helping hand down from the wagon. As he released his hands from her waist, she held onto his arms. "Thank you, Declan, for defending me."

He smiled down at her and kissed her mouth. It was one of the sweetest kisses he'd ever had, filled with emotion of all kind. "You are worthy of that eagle feather," he murmured. "He honored you and…" He reached into his shirt pocket. "I'd be honored if you'd wear this again." He opened his hand to reveal her wedding ring. Nodding, she extended her hand to him, and he slipped the gold band onto her finger where it belonged. "You do me proud, *grá mo chroí.*" He kissed her again, hard and fast.

She laughed as she pulled away. "They'll leave us behind, you know, if we're not packed."

"It might be worth it to be alone with you." Great delight washed over him at her crimson blush.

"I doubt we're overloaded, since we aren't carrying as much as we were before the Platte crossing." He studied their wagon with a critical eye. "But I'm sure the captain will be around to let us know."

They finished eating and packing, and he was right; Captain London and his scouts went from wagon to wagon. There were many loud voices and women crying. When he reached their wagon, Captain London seemed glad to take the offered coffee and a moment to sit.

"It happens every trip." He took a sip and sighed in appreciation. "People think it will happen to someone else, never to them. *Other people* will lose their animals and *their* wagons will fall apart. They think their water is endless." He drained his cup. "I'm sorry to be a bother. Your wagon looks good. You two can lead today if you can start the line right away. Remember, Luella, you'll have to walk."

"I know, Captain. I'm ready."

He handed her the empty cup and tipped his hat to her.

IT WAS GOING to be a long, hot dusty day, but she was ready. She had vinegar and flour in her basket and planned to see who needed what. She'd bet more people than admitted to it drank the water. There were many faces she hadn't seen all morning, though, and she was growing concerned for them.

"What are you up to?" Declan asked, amused.

"I have vinegar and flour in my basket. People are sick, but they have asked no one for help. They just seem to be missing. I thought I'd walk and offer anyone who wants a cure for the alkali poisoning. It's not as near fatal as dysentery, but it's as painful."

"Are you sure you're up to tangling with some of these people?"

"My spirit might be bruised, but it is far from being broken. I still do not know what I have done, but I figure I can be more mindful of helping others. We have been so blessed to have a wagon."

"Don't overdo."

A wider smile had never graced her face. He really cared. "I won't." She felt suddenly shy.

"Wagons Ho!"

She stayed next to their wagon for a bit and then dropped back. It was easy to tell by the awful smell if there was sickness within each wagon. Many folks had their own supplies and thanked her for her advice. A few had her mix the concoction up and drank it down. It wasn't the most pleasant tasting thing to drink, but it aided with the painful symptoms. She felt good about herself, being able to help people.

"It's not going to work, you know."

She didn't even look to see who was behind her. At one time it would have been a sullen Zander giving her grief, but he seemed to keep more to himself these days. "Heath, please leave me alone. I don't want to come between you and your brother."

He snorted. "That's a good game you're playing. You haven't apologized to me once for all you've done."

She stopped, and the horse came dangerously close to running her over. "All *I* have done? Please Heath, list these sins I have committed because I don't know what I've done to earn your ire."

"You don't know the first thing about being a wife. You don't share a bed with your husband, and that is the main wifely duty. You interfere when you shouldn't, and you made my family a laughingstock. People laugh behind your back, and more importantly, behind Declan's back. I don't know where he'll end up settling when we get to Oregon. It'll have to be far away from anyone in this party if he expects to be respected." He kicked the sides of his horse and rode away.

Stunned, she stood in place as other people just walked around her. What was she thinking? She had to get away from these people. One minute she was so happy, and the next she was beyond despair. Even though her life had been difficult, she'd never felt such despair before her father kicked her out of his wagon.

She swallowed hard and, holding her basket close to her, she walked on—alone. She no longer had it in her to offer her cure. Others probably knew about it anyway. Her grandmother had taught her that recipe. So, she'd just keep to herself from now on. If a body didn't care it wouldn't hurt.

The white alkali on top of the sand was blowing harder, and it felt like tiny pieces of glass slashing her skin. The wagons were corralling, but they looked to be so far away. How had she come to be so far behind? She held her head low and watched where she walked. It would stop soon. It was as though she was walking two steps and pushed back one. It was getting difficult to breathe, but with determination she'd get there. Looking up to see how far away the wagons were, she cringed as sharp sand cut into one of her eyes and then she couldn't see much of anything. She rolled into a ball and put her arms over her head, hoping the wind wound die down soon.

But it only blew harsher and more fiercely. The land was so flat there was nowhere to hide. She heard horses, and people yelled out names of others they were looking for, but her name hadn't been called. She just hoped no one would trample her. Finally, she heard Declan.

She stood and threw her arm over her eyes. "I'm here! Declan! Declan!"

No response came. Had the wind taken her words away?

But he was at her side a moment later. With efficient movements, he wrapped a cloth around her eyes and then led her to his horse. He climbed on then grabbed her arm. "Sit behind me so I can block the worst of it," he shouted, and she just barely heard the words over the roaring wind.

She put her foot on top of his in the stirrup and she swung her leg over the horse's back. Before long, she was settled with her arms around his waist and her face buried against his back. It was a short ride, and then she hopped off and Declan followed.

"Get inside the wagon," he yelled, and helped her up and in. "I need to take care of the horse. Cinch the canvas if you can."

The wagon swayed mightily in the fierce wind. She put just a corner of a cloth into their precious water and washed around her eyes so she could see more easily. Then she cinched up the canvas. Her face burned as did her arms and hands. She wished she had her vinegar; it might have taken the sting away, but she'd left her basket out on the trail, and there was nothing for it now. She decided it was an emergency and she put her cup into the water barrel and filled it. She drank it slowly, delighting in the wetness of it. Fearfulness for Declan was edging into her consciousness when he came through the front of the wagon.

"The sand hurts like the very devil." He cinched the front end and made sure the canvas was tightened down. Then he took off his leather gloves and lowered the cloth that covered his mouth and nose. Gently, he cradled her face in his hands. "You must be feeling a world of hurt. It hit so suddenly, and I couldn't find you. I never thought you'd be that far back. Then I thought you might have been given a ride by someone else. I'm glad I kept going, though, so grateful I found you. It was smart to curl up the way you did."

"I... I fell behind," she choked out.

He kissed her cheek. "I'll get the witch hazel to put on your pretty skin." As he turned from her, he said, "Take your dress off. You can cover yourself with a quilt."

She smiled. He knew her so well. She took her dress off and the difference between her exposed skin and non-exposed skin was like night and day. "I looked burned."

Declan turned back and used a clean cloth to wipe her skin with the witch hazel. That soothed her skin, and the way he looked at her soothed her heart.

"We've only had a few peaceful moments since we've been married," she murmured. "I wish we'd been busy making good memories instead of being constantly unsettled. Declan, I know you love someone else. You were truthful about it from the first. You can't turn love off—or on, for that matter." She offered a shaky smile that she didn't feel. "I want to reassure you we'll part once we reach Oregon. You can have your dream of working with Heath and Zander. I also think it best that when we talk, we do it so no one can hear us and mistake what we are saying. I have come across as a harpy, and that leaves you to be the weak husband. I never meant to get between you and your family. The three of you share a unique family love, and I'm not part of it and that's fine. I can't make people like me. I don't want you to go one way and your brother and your friend the other. That's not your dream. Having me a part of your family will just bring everyone shame, and it will make it hard for Heath and Zander to find decent wives."

He opened his mouth and drew a breath.

"Before you say anything—" She held up a hand. "— just know I've made my peace with it. God will show me my path. I have faith that I will be just fine."

"You think people will believe we haven't lain together? It doesn't work that way."

"Heath knows, and he told me I wasn't doing my wifely duty."

"What else did my brother have to say?"

"He's mad that I never apologized to him for all the trouble I've caused. He said I made you and your family a laughingstock and no one will respect you when we get to Oregon." She released a heavy sigh. "You're a good man, Declan Leary, and I will not be your downfall. Even you said I'm more child than woman, and it's true. It must be; because I don't know how to address his accusations. He's really mad about the water."

"You look thin." Declan angled his head and studied her. "Have you been eating?"

"Not as much as usual. I have no appetite, and I think it's the heat. I was thinking I could plead with my father to take me back." A big gust of wind tipped the wagon a bit, and she grabbed onto Declan. "I don't want to die."

"I think we'll be fine." He laid a hand over one of hers as the wagon settled again. "Listen. You will not talk to your father. I have love in my heart for Alana still but I also said goodbye to her, and I know she'd understand. You haven't made me weak. In fact, I feel stronger when I have you near. I wish people would stop their wagging tongues, but you've done nothing wrong. My brother has his knickers in a twist because of the water. He doesn't take kindly to being told what to do. Lord knows you should have been welcomed by both Heath and Zander, and I don't know what's gotten into the pair of them." He pulled her onto his lap. "But I'm not sorry we married. I never thought about looking for a wife, but here you are, and I'm not giving you back." He shifted and took her hands in his. "What if my dreams have changed? What if they include you now? I know we could make a good life for ourselves and any children we are blessed with."

Her mouth opened and he covered it with his own, kissing her until she tingled from head to toe. He pulled back and looked at her.

"The wind has died down," she said softly.

"So it has."

"I say we hang 'im!" a man outside bellowed.

"Oh, dear. I guess we'd better get out there," she said.

Declan ran his thumb over her lips. "Yes, let's go."

Declan climbed out first and lifted her down and this time his touch meant so much more to her. They held hands as they walked into the circle of the wagons. One wagon tilted lying partially on top of another wagon. The air was heavy with the smell of alkali.

Two men held Tomlin between them. "Caught this one sneaking into the wagons that my girls were in. This time he needs to be taught a lesson!" David Turney told all. He turned his furious gaze on Luella and Declan. "If Luella was still keeping Tomlin happy, he'd have no reason to look at my girls. Etta, Aurora, Lorelei are you all right?"

She stiffened but pretended she was fine.

Declan let go of her hand. "I believe you owe my wife an apology. She had nothing to do with that man. She has more self-respect than to get involved with a man like him. Besides, her father never let her out of his sight. She did all the chores, so I don't know when she would have found the time."

Luella's mother struggled to get free from her husband's grip. She stepped next to Declan. "She never had a moment of peace. My husband worked her from sun up to past sun down. Luella is a good girl, and I'm tired of her name being tossed in the mud. Shame on you all, for gossiping so cruelly about my big-hearted girl!"

Many of the travelers looked ashamed.

"My apologies, ma'am." David Turney had the grace to

look embarrassed as he addressed Luella. "My temper has gotten the better of me. I often saw how hard you worked and knew you didn't deserve to be gossiped about. I want justice though."

Her eyes misted. "Thank you."

Captain London took one look at Tomlin and shook his head. "I told you you'd be left behind. You can wait here for another train to come by. I'm done with you."

"You can't keep me from following you!" Tomlin spat.

"True enough, but if you come near our wagons, you'll be shot. Now get out of here. You'd best be away from us in ten minutes' time." He turned and walked back to his wagon.

"I don't want to watch," Luella said.

Declan led her back to their wagon. "I don't think anything is dust-free. I'd best grease the wheels and oil my firearms." He put his hands on her waist. "But first I think I need a kiss to keep me going."

She laughed but stopped when he kissed her. This man was her heart. And finally some broken places began to heal.

CHAPTER SEVEN

he next day was harder than the one before as far as water and heat went. The amount of livestock that died was criminal. Declan wanted to shake some sense into the people he traveled with. They had refused to lighten their loads, and now they were left wondering what to do when their animals died. Declan had no pity for those who were stuck.

They'd seen everything on the side of the trail from furniture to cook stoves to old moldy flour and rancid bacon. The people who had come before hadn't listened either. Bleached bones of oxen, mules, and horses were scattered about.

All of Harrison's animals had been well cared for. Harrison had an extra water barrel in his wagon for the animals. Things had calmed down between Declan and Heath. Declan felt like he could breathe again. Plus his wife smiled at him often.

He looked back, and she was walking with her basket that one of the scouts had found. Cora and Essie were now helping Luella pass out the cure. Luella told him she could smell sickness in some wagons, but the drivers continued to deny it. But why? They couldn't figure. Maybe they were too proud to take the help offered.

The wagons ahead had come to a halt. Declan waited for a scout to ride down the line and tell them why. Soon Tom Simps rode by and told Declan there were graves to be dug. Luella caught up and Declan gave her a hand up so she could sit on the bench next to him.

"What's happening?"

"Simps said they were digging graves."

She sighed. "I hope they don't have to dig many. It's sad isn't it?" She leaned her head against his shoulder. "I keep thinking about how you defended me yesterday. I'm so proud to be your wife. My heart had been broken and near empty, and now I feel it filling with my love for you and it's the most wonderful thing I've ever experienced." She twisted against him and gazed up. "Especially since I trust you not to break it again. I want that dream of yours. I want the land, the horses and cattle. I want to have your children. I can picture our children playing with Heath and Zander's children. So you see my love, you are now stuck with me." Her face glowed.

He started leaning to kiss her, but they got the signal to circle up. He squeezed her hand. "Let's just pray it's not as bad as I think it is."

He drove the wagon into place and helped Luella down. Hand in hand, they went to an area where graves were being dug. There were five already dug.

"Oh, no," she said as she covered her mouth.

One whole family of four, plus three children from another family and two adults. It was sad.

"I tried to help that family, but they told me to go away," she told Declan when she learned their names. "I didn't know about the rest." She nodded at the men with shovels. "They are digging even more graves."

Declan glanced over, saw who they were carrying to the graves before she did, and pulled her into an embrace, cradling her face against his shoulder. She struggled to find out what he was protecting her from, and when she did see, she sagged against him.

"No! Oh, Declan why? It can't be. Not all of them. They knew I could help them but… why didn't they just ask?"

He swung her up into his arms and started to carry her back to their wagon.

"No, I need to see them properly buried." Her body shook as tears streamed down her face. "We just saw my mother. She was fine."

His heart wrenched for her grief. "We'll say a few words over them. Come and rest for a bit."

"Please put me down. I must—I need…"

He set her on her feet, and with his arm wrapped around her waist, walked her to the graves where her entire family was being lowered.

"At the dawn of this day, I was positive nothing could ruin my day. I was the luckiest woman alive," she whispered through her tears. "Who knew what grief this day held for me? I have lost my family, and though I was ready to never talk to my father again, I never would have chosen his death."

"They are with God now. It doesn't stop the hurt, I know it doesn't."

Cora came running and hugged Luella then held her as she cried. Harrison stood next to them all, looking the way Declan felt, helpless.

Declan wanted to curse the fates, but it would do no good. There was no changing things. He knew grief, Lord knew he knew grief. So he'd help her through it as best as he could. In time, after she mourned, he'd have his sweet glowing wife again. In a long time. He sighed and took Luella into his arms. She held on so tight. He could feel her need of him to be strong. He could do that, be there for her, supporting her. That could be his redemption to her.

The graves were covered with dirt, and the reverend said a few words. It was probably much more than a few but Declan couldn't seem to pay attention. In the distance, he could see a great rock. He'd always know where they were buried.

———

THERE WASN'T ENOUGH for a proper goodbye. So much wasted time. She hadn't talked to her brothers in what seemed like forever. They hadn't tried to talk to her, but she had understood that no one had wanted to cross her father. The saddest part was giving their wagon away. Luella didn't have much time to take what she wanted out of it. She kept a couple of books that belonged to her brothers and her mother's trunk along with a few tapestries she had needle pointed. She almost left her father's pocket watch behind, but in the end, she took it.

They kept the food and half the water and made arrangements for the oxen and wagon to be returned once they got to Oregon. People went through the belongings she left behind while the new owners put their own things into the wagon. She tried not to look, but it was impossible. She gasped when she saw the piano.

She ran and stood between the wagon and the piano. "No."

"Get out of the way, you loose skirt," the eldest man said.

She drew herself up straight and tall. "Didn't you ask yourself why did my oxen die while my wagon broke apart until it was useless?"

"It's not your business. Now stand aside," the man practically growled. "This doesn't belong to you. It belongs to your husband. You have no say."

She felt Declan's heartening presence next to her.

"She has a say. My wife is very wise, and she's usually right. I'm dumbfounded that you think you can have those beasts haul your heavy piano over the deserts and mountains and everything in between. Did you take care of your livestock?"

Captain London cleared his voice loudly. "Leave the piano behind and you will make sure this wagon and the oxen are in good condition upon our arrival in Oregon or you'll pay for it. Understood?"

The man stared for a long time. At last, he spat on the ground and answered, "Understood."

She walked away. She didn't want to hear any phony apologies from the overbearing man. Her eyes were now surprisingly dry, and she just wanted to get going. She had been promised clear water at the end of the day and she *would* be taking a bath. Would she ever be able to get all the sand and dust out of the wagon? Maybe they'd sleep in the tent tonight. It might be cooler. If she could just lie in the circle of his arms, she'd be fine.

"I'm proud of you, my little meek as a mouse wife." Declan kissed her forehead.

"I thought I'd end up under the piano." She chuckled. "I really did. Thank you for standing up for me."

"I stood beside you. That's as it should be." He gestured to the wagon. "Let's get you up on the bench."

"I'm supposed to walk."

"Usually, but I want you with me. It's unusual circumstances, and I want to be sure you are all right."

She nodded.

"Do you see that large rock in the distance? It's Independence Rock. It's said if you are there by the Fourth of July, you'll make it through the mountains just fine without getting snowed on."

"It's only June, isn't it? I'm not sure of the exact date."

"It's June eleventh. The plan is to stop at the rock. From what I gather, it's a time for celebration. Of course we won't considering we just buried your family."

She stared at the rock. It was massive. The Lord certainly knew how to decorate. She had prayed for the souls of her mother and two brothers, but she couldn't bring herself to pray for her father and she felt shamed. She'd pray again later and include him.

"You're alive one day and gone the next. That's just the way of it. It seems to me one should grab happiness while they can. Would it be unseemly to watch the celebration? In my own way I've been grieving for my family since the day my father made me leave. I kept hoping that my mother or brothers would let me know they still loved me through a look or a note even but they refused to look at me even when my father had gone hunting. It's been hard and I foolishly kept waiting. The wait is over, but the hurt had changed to grief."

"It'll be a long day, but the spring water valley is down there at the rock. I haven't forgotten that you want a bath tonight, *grá mo chroí*."

"You might as well slow down so I can get off."

"Be careful."

She smiled. "I will." She jumped as soon as the wagon came to a crawl. She took one last look at the area where her family was buried. Then she turned and looked in front of her, toward the future. She needed tell Declan how very much she loved him.

She walked alone this time only because she wanted to. She wanted to remember how her family used to be. She said goodbye to each of them and prayed again for their souls to be welcomed in heaven. They'd live in her heart forever. They hadn't always been so cold.

Maybe she wasn't hurting as she should or maybe she'd been hurting for too long. She needed to concentrate on Declan now, on their marriage. Just thinking about him had her smiling.

There was supposed to be water at the base of Independence Rock. She swore she could smell the water well before she saw it. Imagine how many people had come to the same spot. She'd heard hundreds of names and initials had been carved in the rock, and she wanted to see some of them. The rock itself was huge. From a distance, she felt it looked turtle shaped, but as they grew closer, it was impossible to see the whole thing. Was it possible that she could feel anticipation in the air? Everyone around her seemed relieved to get out of the arid sand.

Oscar Randolf, one scout she'd not known well, was riding down the line. She heard him tell everyone to get into their wagons and for the drivers to have a firm hand on the lines. The livestock might try to bolt to the Sweetwater River, and someone could get hurt.

The wagons all slowed, and she hurried and caught up with Declan. He smiled as he gave her his hand and helped her up.

"I will have a tight rein on these oxen. I have a feeling a few of the foolish people won't be holding on hard enough and there will be chaos. Hold on to the wagon seat."

"It sounds like a good plan. I can't wait to get clean. I do believe some of the sand has become part of my skin. I need a good scrubbing."

"Let me know if you need help... with the scrubbing part." He grinned at her.

"You are shameless, Declan Leary. But shameless or not,

you're a blessing from God so I'll just have to teach you how to be normal." She laughed.

"Normal? What is normal? Would that be normal for an American or for an Irishman? You do know that the Irish are a race and our ancestors were kings and great warriors."

"Mine were great worriers."

Declan laughed. "I like us this way, comfortable with each other. I'd take your hand, but I'm holding the lines."

"And kiss me?" she asked shyly, sending him a sidelong glance, unable to hide the smile teasing her lips.

"Well now, I'd say — Hang on!" He gripped the reins tighter.

All around them, people broke from the line and their wagons were going willy-nilly, far too fast with drivers no longer in control.

"They didn't hold tight enough," she yelled above the loud noise of the animals. She held on so tight to the seat and the wagon side her fingers went numb. She could only hope they didn't get knocked over. Soon enough, they were one of the few left who had control of their livestock.

"Oh, no! Look, a wagon tipped into the river!"

Declan nodded and let the oxen begin a slow walk to the river. "Looks like it's that Eddie's wagon that went into the water."

"Isn't he the one who treated Cora so horribly? I don't feel too sorry for him then."

Declan nodded. "I believe in second chances, but some people want third and fourth chances. I have a feeling God's hand nudged him in."

Her breath caught at his matter-of-fact comment. "Could be. Look, the water is supposed to be clear!" She stared at the murky muddy mess where animals that had broken free were milling about and filling up on water and made a face.

Then she pointed in the other direction. "At least it is upstream."

"That's where I'm heading. The water is pretty stirred up where the rest of them raced to." Silence fell for a moment as he steered the wagon toward the river. Then he said almost shyly, "There'll be a dance tonight. I was wondering if you'd do me the honor of allowing me to escort you to it."

Happiness blossomed in her heart. "I'd be delighted. You know I'm not much of a dancer. But you are."

"Darlin, I'm Irish. We're born dancing. And I'll be happy to show you." They came to a stop. "Stay on the wagon." He tied off the brake and jumped down then unyoked the anxious oxen and led them to the water.

Pride welled up in her chest. He was a fine husband.

———

SHE HAD BEEN SAVING the new dress that had been given to her when she'd nearly drowned, and as soon as she put the aqua colored dress on she felt pretty. It was a wonderful sensation. But it was more than the dress. Her husband had her thinking she might not be as plain as she had thought.

It had been a full day. Declan helped her climb Independence Rock, and they carved their initials in it. Then she took her long desired bath and scrubbed herself while Declan made sure no one peeked in at her. Now she was dressed for the dance. After taking a deep breath, she went to the back of the wagon and Declan was just outside in new clothes awaiting her. He reached up for her and she leaned into him and wrapped her arms around his neck.

As he set her down, she stole a kiss. She unwound her arms, but he pulled her closer and kissed her back.

"You're so beautiful."

Her face heated. "It's the dress."

"Now I'm not one to be disagreeing with my wife, but a mere dress wouldn't make you beautiful inside and out." His eyes twinkled with pure joy that was certainly echoed in her heart. "We'll be meeting Zander and Heath at the dance. They have guard duty in a few hours."

Puzzled, she furrowed her brow. "Why haven't you had guard duty?"

"I was supposed to, but they offered to take longer turns so I could be with you. I'm not sure exactly how it happened but we're set to live near each other again." A grin spread across his face. "And no one had better say a thing about you in front of them. Heath already punched one drover when he said something impolite."

She smiled at him. "I don't believe in violence, but maybe that one time."

"You're an imp." He offered her his arm. "Ready, Mrs. Leary?"

She wrapped her hand around his strong bicep and nodded, too choked up by it all to speak. She gave him a light squeeze. He looked proud to have her on his arm and it amazed her he'd feel that way. Then again, he did want everyone to think they were happy, so they'd stop talking about them.

"Is something worrying you?" He stopped and gazed deep into her eyes.

"No. I'm just nervous."

He took her hand and led her into the crowd of dancers. "This is a nice slow one to start out with."

Somehow she didn't know they'd be dancing so close to each other. She concentrated and when she had the steps down she glanced up and the look in his eye melted her heart. He held her close for the rest of the song.

As the group of fiddles and the solitary harmonica started a more lively beat, he hung back a bit, though he nodded his head in rhythm. "This next one is pretty fast. Why don't we watch first?" He led her to the edge of the dancing. "Will you take a walk with me?" The look on his face was serious.

"Of course." Her heart began to drum hard against her chest. She took his offered hand and they walked a while along the river.

"It's a beautiful evening, and I wanted to talk to you, alone." He dropped her hand and took a blanket out from under a bush.

She inhaled sharply as a wave of pleasure washed over her. He'd had this planned. He helped her to sit and then he sat close to her. "You don't need to look doubtful."

"I don't know what to think."

"That's the problem. We came together in a very unconventional way. And we were forced to marry. I have to admit I wasn't happy about it at the time. I'm a man who likes to make his own decisions."

Tears filled her eyes. It was kinder to know that he didn't want her, truly it was. She'd have time to make other arrangements this way. That had been the deal she had offered in the first place, after all. He still loved Alana—hadn't he told her as much?—and she didn't blame him. Folks couldn't just stop loving someone. Though she had thought...

"My life has been filled with joy and heartbreak and then joy again. I never thought to feel this way," he admitted.

"Please stop. Our deal still holds. You won't be responsible for me once we get to Oregon. You're right, of course."

"Why am I right?" His voice was practically a whisper.

"You were made for better than the likes of me. You love Alana, and I don't fit. Heath and Zander might agree to live near you now, but they were so set against me that I'm afraid I'll say the wrong thing and you'll be out on your own again. You never planned on me and you're right they forced you to marry me. I'm not afraid. God is always with me. He will protect me."

His jaw dropped. He pulled her closer and wiped away her tears with the pads of his thumbs. "You are my *a mhuirnín, grá mo chroí*. You are my darling, the love of my heart."

She lifted her gaze to his. "You say *grá mo chroí* to me all the time. Is it true? Am I the love of your heart?"

"Yes, you are. I love you with my whole being. I love seeing your beautiful face in the morning and your sweet smiles through the day. On occasion, I see admiration in your eyes as though you find me pleasing as well. At night, I like to know that I can hold you in my arms and that you are mine. I look forward to a future with you. I thought you knew, but now I also see doubt in your eyes. I want to be sure you know that you are the breath I breathe, you are the light I see by, you are my willingness to keep going, and you are the excitement in my life. Most of all you are my greatest blessing from God, and it humbles me he entrusted someone so precious to my care."

"I love you too." Her voice shook. "I'm not as well-expressed with words the way you are. But you make me feel worthy and joyful. I've never felt this way about anyone before, and I thank God that I have you."

"Would you do me the grand honor of making this marriage real?" There was so much love in his eyes.

"Yes, oh yes."

"Good, hopefully when we turn in for the night. Though who knows if we'll end up with privacy."

Her face heated. "I want us to have a family. Nothing would make me happier."

"Don't you worry. That's the plan. We can get a lot of land since we're married. I imagine cattle and horses grazing on our land. We'll check the soil and grow some crops. We'll have a garden and by canning what we grow we'll have food all winter. I bet there are berries for jam too."

"What about a house?" she asked.

A smile played around his lips. "Your face is all aglow when we talk about the future. I want to make it big enough to hold everyone for holiday get-togethers. I want it bright and cheerful and a place where people want to be. A place where children can play while the adults relax. Best of all, there will be no rents to pay and no one can come and set us out. There will be no fear of nationwide hunger. I can speak Gaelic if I like and I can practice my religion without being afraid of soldiers storming us. I won't have to see my friends die out in the road of starvation." His voice broke and he drew a deep breath before he went on. "I'll be considered a free man, in a free country. We were never free in Ireland. England thought they knew what was best for us and gave our land away to their peerage, leaving us to say yes sir and yes ma'am. They decided we were an inferior race. One day they will see how wrong they are. We've held on to our traditions and music and language despite it all being against the law. All of their rules strengthened us and we yearned more and more for what we used to have. It's beautiful there, Luella and it near broke my heart to leave it behind. Men and women were being shipped off in convict ships for the crime of stealing an ear of corn to feed their babes.

"It didn't matter if you worked hard. There wasn't any food. But you know what I think? I believe if they think they own my country then they had a responsibility to see that we were all fed. The government wanted to be part of everything else we did, but when we started dying off, where were they? They ran a program to build roads, but they didn't have jobs for everyone, and the weakest were given the jobs and they died right there on the road with a shovel in their hands because the mere pittance they were paid wasn't enough to pay for food. The price was beyond most of our means. God help me, but it was as if they wanted us dead. They had no use for us except to serve them. It happened again and again and again." He raised his chin. "But no more. Our children will laugh, learn, and work on land we own. I'll be able to hunt for food and not be in fear of being hanged for poaching. There will be no need to steal to feed our babes."

A longing deep inside stirred as he mentioned feeding their babes. She had much to say herself, but she sensed he was not yet finished.

"We've always been proud, but we weren't always allowed to stand tall. I stand tall now as do my brother and Zander. There aren't soldiers to beat us down at every turn. Our children will be free and for that, I am overjoyed. No one will be able to kick in our door and search our house or burn our house down. Best of all I will have you beside me, loving me and for that I am grateful."

Tears filled her eyes, spilled over, and still she let him talk, needing to hear him as much as he needed to say the words.

"Our life will be one of love and wonder. And you will forever be *a mhuirnín, grá mo chroí.*"

"You, my husband, are a brave and passionate man. God blessed me the day I got run over. Come teach me how to dance some more. It's a grand evening."

He pulled her to him and kissed her. "I know you'll be a fast learner." He took her hand and entwined their fingers together and then led her back into the light.

THANK you for reading Luella's Longing. The journey of Harrison, Cora, Declan and Luella continues in book three. I've gotten comments about the book not being finished. They are not stand alone books. But I do understand the frustration. Amazon rewards writers who publish quickly.

They show those books more and give them a nudge up. I hope it works. I'm trying to only allow two weeks between books. Please if you are so inclined leave a review. I can get better advertising quicker if I have reviews. I appreciate all of you who have taken the time to read my books.

THE END

I'm so pleased you chose to read Luella's Longing, and it's my sincere hope that you enjoyed the story. I would appreciate if you'd consider posting a review. This can help an author tremendously in obtaining a readership. My many thanks. ~ Kathleen

ABOUT THE AUTHOR

Sexy Cowboys and the Women Who Love Them...
Finalist in the 2012 and 2015 RONE Awards.
Top Pick, Five Star Series from the Romance Review.
Kathleen Ball writes contemporary and historical western
romance with great emotion and
memorable characters. Her books are award winners and
have appeared on best sellers lists including: Amazon's Best
Seller's List, All Romance Ebooks, Bookstrand, Desert
Breeze Publishing and Secret Cravings Publishing Best
Sellers list. She is the recipient of eight Editor's Choice
Awards, and The Readers' Choice Award for Ryelee's
Cowboy.
Winner of the Lear diamond award Best Historical Novel-
Cinders' Bride
There's something about a cowboy

facebook.com/kathleenballwesternromance

twitter.com/kballauthor

instagram.com/author_kathleenball

OTHER BOOKS BY KATHLEEN

Lasso Spring Series

Callie's Heart

Lone Star Joy

Stetson's Storm

Dawson Ranch Series

Texas Haven

Ryelee's Cowboy

Cowboy Season Series

Summer's Desire

Autumn's Hope

Winter's Embrace

Spring's Delight

Mail Order Brides of Texas

Cinder's Bride

Keegan's Bride

Shane's Bride

Tramp's Bride

Poor Boy's Christmas

Oregon Trail Dreamin'

We've Only Just Begun

A Lifetime to Share

A Love Worth Searching For

So Many Roads to Choose

The Settlers

Greg

Juan

Scarlett

Mail Order Brides of Spring Water

Tattered Hearts

Shattered Trust

Glory's Groom

Battered Soul

Romance on the Oregon Trail

Cora's Courage

Luella's Longing

Dawn's Destiny

Terra's Trial

The Greatest Gift

Love So Deep

Luke's Fate

Whispered Love

Love Before Midnight

I'm Forever Yours

Finn's Fortune

Glory's Groom

Printed in Great Britain
by Amazon